"A thoughtful, moving exploration of a horrific murder from the point of view of how it affected many of the people surrounding the story ... Deveau has created a play that is complex, layered, compassionate, and not a cut-and-dried look at a terrible crime."
—LYNN SLOTKIN, The Slotkin Letter

"The characters in *My Funny Valentine* are compelling and nuanced. Their distances from the action allow what could have been a straightforward real-life horror story to unfold like a murder mystery, a whydunit where the answer will never make sense."
—MARK LEIREN-YOUNG, *Vancouver Sun*

"An exceptionally beautiful piece of work ... Meticulously scripted characters shot through with contradictions ... Simply superb."
—JO LEDINGHAM, *Vancouver Courier*

"With *My Funny Valentine*, Deveau proves himself once again as a playwright on the rise."
—MARK ROBINS, Gay Vancouver

FOR *LADIES AND GENTLEMEN, BOYS AND GIRLS*

Nominated for three Dora Mavor Moore Awards, including for Outstanding New Play

"Often when we talk about differences, empathy, and inclusion, the conversations can become abstract and intellectual. [*Ladies and Gentlemen, Boys and Girls*] invoked a much more grounded sense of empathy and understanding of the challenges students and their families face when kids identify their own differences. Beautifully written."
—Toronto District School Board

CISSY

THREE GENDER PLAYS

Nelly Boy

My Funny Valentine

and

Ladies and Gentlemen, Boys and Girls

by Dave Deveau

With a preface by the author

TALONBOOKS

Talonbooks
9259 Shaughnessy Street, Vancouver, British Columbia, Canada V6P 6R4
talonbooks.com

Talonbooks is located on xʷməθkʷəy̓əm, Sḵwx̱wú7mesh, and səl̓ilwətaʔɬ Lands.

First printing: 2020

Typeset in Arno
Printed and bound in Canada on 100% post-consumer recycled paper
Cover by andrea bennett, interior by Typesmith

Cover photography by Paola Rizzi, www.photopierre.it, © Paola Rizzi, used with permission

Talonbooks acknowledges the financial support of the Canada Council for the Arts, the Government of Canada through the Canada Book Fund, and the Province of British Columbia through the British Columbia Arts Council and the Book Publishing Tax Credit.

LIBRARY AND ARCHIVES CANADA CATALOGUING IN PUBLICATION

Title: Cissy : three gender plays ; Nelly boy ; My funny Valentine, and ; Ladies and gentlemen, boys and girls / by Dave Deveau.

Other titles: Plays. Selections | Nelly boy | My funny Valentine | Ladies and gentlemen, boys and girls

Names: Deveau, Dave, author. | Container of (work): Deveau, Dave. Nelly boy. | Container of (work): Deveau, Dave. My funny Valentine. | Container of (work): Deveau, Dave. Ladies and gentlemen, boys and girls.

Identifiers: Canadiana 20190153911 | ISBN 9781772012521 (SOFTCOVER)

Classification: LCC PS8607.E93 A6 2020 | DDC C812/.6—dc23

To Janina and Dennis for the past

To Cameron for the present

To Dexter for the future

CONTENTS

PREFACE

BY DAVE DEVEAU

I love plays. I love the kinds of conversations they crack open, and the kinds of spaces they enable us to inhabit.

Michel Tremblay was my gateway into the world of theatre. When I first saw a production of *Les Belles-Sœurs* at the Great Canadian Theatre Company in Ottawa (under the direction of Micheline Chevrier) I was floored by the power of seeing fifteen women onstage and knew immediately that I wanted to pursue playwriting. I had written in other forms, and pursued acting throughout my childhood, but this play catalyzed my desire to help tell the stories of the people I surrounded myself with, and the communities I was part of.

Many years later, I was working as an usher at Toronto's Harbourfront Centre and had the good fortune of catching Theatre Direct and Theaturtle's production of *Alphonse* by Wajdi Mouawad (directed by Lynda Hill and Alon Nashman). The show had a perfect performance alchemy: exquisite writing of tremendous appeal to children, but was also a vital, mesmerizing theatrical experience for adults. I wrote a letter to Lynda Hill thanking her for this transformative experience, and telling her I'd love to learn and grow and work with the company. I had the gall to send her a script that I'd been working on, titled *The Fat Kid Dreams*; seeing *Alphonse* had provided another eureka moment, a realization that I wanted to create plays for young people. *The Fat Kid Dreams* was not a wonderful script, but it signalled the beginning of what would become an ongoing conversation with younger audiences – I received a phone call from Marjorie Chan, then playwright-in-residence with Theatre Direct, inviting me to a playwrights' discussion group. I was shocked and deeply thrilled. On the day of the discussion group, I made my way from North York to their offices beside the Randolph Academy for the Performing Arts, just beside Mirvish Village, with every intention to discuss ... something. I didn't know what. But I was ready to fake it until I made it. Except that day there was a massive storm, and not many people were able to show up. But I was able to chat with Marjorie and Lynda, and discover that they were interested in commissioning me to be part of a group of playwrights (including Marjorie, Lisa Codrington, Soraya Peerbaye, and myself), who would each explore themes of democracy for a project that eventually became *The Demonstration*. I knew I'd write about the democracy of gender, something that wasn't much on the radar yet on that day in 2003. The monologue I created for *The Demonstration* became the basis for *Nelly Boy*. Theatre Direct continued to support me, with additional help from the Ontario Arts Council, as I fleshed it out into a full play. *Nelly Boy* premiered in 2009 as the second production for Zee Zee Theatre, a Vancouver theatre company founded by my husband Cameron Mackenzie, which is mandated to amplify voices from the margins.

As I reread *Nelly Boy*, revising it for inclusion in this book, I am amazed, or maybe disheartened, to see that it still feels current. This isn't to say that the world hasn't changed – since 2003, twenty-two countries have entrenched legal protections for transgender people, and in Canada public bathrooms are slowly becoming more accessible to trans and gender-variant folks – but there is still a lot of changing left to do. Statistics surrounding violence against trans women continue to be alarmingly and disproportionately high. Even factions of the queer community are dividing over who has access to gendered spaces.

My husband and I are drag queens. We raise our little boy in a house full of costumes, and sequins, and endless books. We perform for each other constantly. Our best friend often accuses us of dressing, in our day-to-day form, as Batman villains – endless colour and distracting pattern. We do not fit within a lot of gender narratives. For me, creating the character of Nelly started an ongoing journey in writing for voices who don't fit into binarist gender. This writing journey is a process of allyship, which I recognize to be lifelong; it involves building relationships based on trust, consistency, and accountability. It's about having difficult conversations, about learning and relearning and challenging oneself and others. About putting privilege to good use, and amplifying other voices whenever possible.

In February 2008 I tuned into the *Ellen DeGeneres Show* to get my fix of mindless daytime whimsy. I was surprised, instead, to find an unusually sombre Ellen speaking in direct address to the camera about a fifteen-year-old boy who had asked another boy in his class to be his valentine, only to have that boy bring a gun to school and shoot him in the face the next day. I was immediately distraught: crying, irrational, angry that the first time I'd heard about this boy was not from the news but from a daytime talk show. And I became obsessive. I read everything I could, and I started collecting materials in a binder – not because I was intending to write the boy's story, at least not at first, but because it was an event that shook me to my core, and I had no choice but to delve deeper in order to come up with any kind of sense as to how or why this boy's murder had taken place. Eventually this research manifested into writing that I described as a conversation I wanted to have with an audience, in person. As myself, Dave. I conducted this theatrical experiment, called *My Funny Valentine*, in the backspace of Theatre Passe Muraille as part of the 2009 SummerWorks Performance Festival. It was a complicated experience, especially given that the preliminary hearings were happening in real time with our rehearsal process. I was doing rewrites on the fly as new details emerged about the case. As I continued digging, slowly but surely, through a lot of development and hard decisions, a play emerged, which Zee Zee Theatre premiered in 2011. As the case continued developing alongside the play, I rewrote the final monologue (which takes place in the present), including a new one for the 2013 remount, and again re-envisioning it for our ten-year-anniversary production in 2018. The murder of Lawrence (Latisha) Fobes King has now been the inspiration for many works of both fiction and non-fiction, and *My Funny Valentine* is one these. The play asks difficult, and often unanswerable questions from a spectrum of people affected by the murder, all played by a single actor, and all over the course of eighty short minutes.

The final play in this volume, *Ladies and Gentlemen, Boys and Girls*, was created in response to social conservatism in my now-home province of British Columbia. In October 2014, after the Vancouver School Board brought in new, more inclusive policies surrounding Sexual Orientation and Gender Identity (SOGI), a group of parents took the school board to the Supreme Court of British Columbia, believing that these new policies violated charter rights. The parents (and some politicians too) believed that trans students should not be permitted to use a washroom or change room of their choice, and believed that, as parents, they should be informed by the school of their child's gender-related behaviours. With that backdrop in the city where I live, I very much wanted to bring a frank story about trans experience to young audiences. Children are brilliant. Their minds are open and keen to connect to the world, discovering, developing, and questioning opinions and beliefs. When I play with my son – when we have our daily dance parties, or when I take him somewhere new and I watch him try to memorize the terrain, try to make sense of every item he encounters through trial and error – I remember that young minds don't get as caught up in the mundane as older brains do. My husband and I are theatre-makers. Our son seems to be gravitating toward sports and cars – wonderful things we know nothing about. He is opening our comfort levels to new things and we are keen to dive in. So in response to these parents I was seeing on television – and in response to how different this was to the structure of my own household and beliefs – I wanted to develop a play about parents who learn from their child, rather than the other way around. And so as a playwright-in-residence at Toronto's Roseneath Theatre, I spent a year developing *Ladies and Gentlemen, Boys and Girls*. The play was met with great feedback, but more important than that was where the play went, and who was able to access it. In addition to the Greater Toronto Area, Roseneath's touring production visited many smaller towns in Northern Ontario, communities that recognized that they have a trans or gender-variant kid and needed a conversation starter in their classrooms. I celebrate the administrators and leaders who demonstrated how integral that conversation might be.

Art exists in response and relationship to the world around it. It asks uncomfortable questions, that can serve as a call to action. These three plays, each in their own way, ask open-ended and vital questions to their audience and, in turn, to you, the reader: How can we passively exist in a world where horrendous injustice remains? Where do we find joy in moments of despair? When do we allow our most fundamental humanity to shine brightest? And, most importantly, what kind of world are we handing over to young people?

Plays are living documents that are only breathed into life when staged in conversation with an audience. But the conversations don't end when the actors bow and the audience applauds – they continue into the lobby, onto the bus, into the car on the way home. They continue replaying in dreams, and eventually, hopefully, they find their way into hearts and minds and remain there, perhaps, ever so slightly and incrementally, changing the very shape of our world.

CISSY

THREE GENDER PLAYS

NELLY BOY

PRODUCTION HISTORY

The original monologue, "Nelly," was commissioned by Theatre Direct Canada and its artistic director Lynda Hill as part of *The Demonstration* (2005–2006 season), directed by Mark Cassidy, with the monologue performed by Frank Cox-O'Connell.

Early versions of this work were published as "Nelly" in *Acting Out: Scenes and Monologues from Theatre Direct Productions for Youth*, edited by Lynda Hill (Toronto: Playwrights Canada Press, 2007), and the University of British Columbia's Journal of Writing for Children's *Chameleon 6* (2008). It was generously supported by the Ontario Arts Council Theatre Creators' Reserve in its development.

Nelly Boy's workshop production took place at the 2007 SummerWorks Performance Festival and was produced by Thirty Below Theatre. It was first produced by Zee Zee Theatre, in association with Screaming Weenie Productions (now the frank theatre company), at the PAL Studio Theatre in Vancouver, British Columbia, from October 22 to November 1, 2009, with the following cast and crew:

NELLY	Amitai Marmorstein
MAN and **FATHER**	Allan Zinyk

Director	Cameron Mackenzie
Assistant Director	Sean Cummings
Set Designer	Marina Szijarto
Costume Designer	Sydney Cavanagh
Lighting Designer	Jergus Oprsal
Sound Designer	Michael Rinaldi
Technical Director	Tim Furness
Stage Manager	Jillian Perry
Movement Coach	Alexis Quednau
Gender Consultant	Gwen Haworth

CHARACTERS

NELLY, fifteen, a genderqueer, non-binary teen

MAN, between thirty and fifty, Nelly's interrogator

FATHER (same actor as **MAN**), Nelly's father

SETTING

A nondescript room, neon-lit and stark, with an implied observation glass.

Amitai Marmorstein as Nelly and Allan Zinyk as Man in Zee Zee Theatre's 2009 premiere production of *Nelly Boy* at PAL Studio Theatre.

Photos by Brandon Gaukel, courtesy of Zee Zee Theatre.

*Lights up. **NELLY** is stark naked, fully
exposed, except for scraps of a torn dress.
Highway traffic sounds. A flash of light.*

Blackout.

*Lights up. A **MAN** sits at a table in a nondescript
room. He stares out at the audience as if through
an observation window. He taps his pencil on the
table, flips the page on his notepad, and waits.*

*NELLY enters, wearing a baggy
sweatsuit and holding a paper bag.*

*Upon seeing the **MAN**, **NELLY** stops.*

NELLY: Oh.

MAN: Oh?

NELLY: I didn't expect ... I didn't know there'd already be ... Well,
someone in here. I figured I'd be left alone for a while.

MAN: Oh. Well, I'm here.

NELLY: I see that.

MAN: Sit.

NELLY sits. Long pause.

MAN: So.

NELLY: So?

MAN: Do you know why you're here?

NELLY: I'm assuming it's not because I won the school raffle. I never have any luck.

MAN: Afraid not. Do you know who I am?

NELLY: Does it matter?

MAN: I suppose not. But if we're going to do it by the book ...

NELLY: Do I look like a by-the-book kind of person?

Pause.

MAN: Well?

NELLY: Well what?

MAN: Are you ready to ...

NELLY: I need a minute.

MAN: Whatever you need.

NELLY: I didn't think there'd be anyone. I thought I'd have time to think.

MAN: You don't need to think, just let it all come out.

NELLY: I'd like to go.

MAN: Where?

NELLY: Somewhere else.

MAN: I'm afraid that's not possible.

NELLY: Why not?

MAN: Because I need to hear what you have to say.

NELLY: Well I'm afraid *that's* not possible.

MAN: Loggerheads already.

NELLY: Mm-hmm.

MAN: You don't want to talk ...

NELLY: I want and don't want a lot of things.

MAN: Like?

NELLY: What everyone else wants.

MAN: And what does everyone want?

NELLY: Have you ever looked into a fishbowl? Just a little goldfish in some kid's bedroom swimming round and around and around and never really getting anywhere, nowhere productive, but relishing in the journey, forgetting about everything else, forgetting everything, letting it all be new, every time, going and going. That's what I want. It's simple, isn't it? To forget it all and keep going, hoping that the next time around it'll all be better.

MAN: Do you want to speak to a social worker?

NELLY: Why?

MAN: I can arrange for a social worker if you'd feel more comfortable.

NELLY: You'll be fine, I guess. Good as anyone. By the book.

MAN: Fishbowl.

NELLY: Always under observation.

MAN: Not always.

> *He looks out at the audience through an implied observation glass.*

Beat.

NELLY: So you want all of it?

MAN: Yes.

NELLY: I don't think that's possible. I'll be exhausted. And I'll need water. Lots of it.

MAN: We can get you water.

Beat.

NELLY: Bottled, hopefully. You have no idea what kind of things can be found in tap water. I've heard horror stories. I can't pay you for the water, mind you, but it would be appreciated anyway. I get parched quickly ...

MAN: Bottled water's not supposed to be so good either. Guess you can't win.

Beat.

NELLY: I'm thirsty.

MAN: That's fine. We'll get you something, just tell me what you remember.

NELLY: What I remember? Well I remember all of it.

NELLY adjusts the sweatsuit.

MAN: Are you uncomfortable?

NELLY: It's alright.

MAN: Good.

NELLY: Kind of big.

MAN: It's what we could do.

> NELLY *adjusts the sleeves of the sweatsuit, rolls them up, then gives up as they slide back down.*

MAN: Is there anything else, or ...?

NELLY: Or?

MAN: Or can we begin?

NELLY: How do you mean?

MAN: Have you had your minute? Are you ready?

NELLY: I still need ...

> NELLY *gestures, suggesting a glass of water.* MAN *exits.*

> NELLY *looks around the room, then opens the paper bag and pulls out the remnants of a dress.* NELLY *takes them in.* NELLY *is transfixed and revisits a memory.*

> MAN *returns holding a small cup of water.*
> NELLY *quickly puts the dress away,*
> *placing the bag under the chair.*

> MAN *hands* NELLY *the tiniest cup of water.*

NELLY: Oh, okay.

> NELLY *turns from him, drinks, crumples the cup, and throws it near* MAN*'s feet.*

> NELLY *still doesn't speak.*

MAN: Fine, you want me to ask the questions? Why do you think you're here?

NELLY: You're not supposed to run along a highway. I know that now. Lesson learned.

MAN: *Does* this have to do with the highway?

NELLY: Are you asking that or leading me into a trap?

MAN: Nobody's trying to trap you. We are all friends here.

NELLY: Friends don't wear such terrible ties.

> *Beat.*

MAN: Would you prefer if I removed it?

NELLY: That would be much appreciated. Yes.

MAN: Tell you what. If I take the tie off, you start your story. Scratch each other's backs a bit.

> *NELLY doesn't respond. MAN removes his tie.*

MAN: Better. Good. Now ... Why are you here?

> *NELLY observes the MAN then turns away from him.*

NELLY: I wake up one morning. I can smell the coffee that my mom has brewed, which means my father is in the shower. That's how it happens, every morning, like clockwork.

Except this is one of those unnerving mornings when my mother, under the weather and souped up on heavy migraine meds, neglects to properly line up the carafe under the filter on the machine, thus coffee has flooded the counter. She hasn't noticed and I'm not going to be the first. That would involve cleaning products and paper towels, and the fumes make me nauseous, and I've sworn off paper towels for the environment's sake.

I creep out into the kitchen, yesterday's clothes on, my backpack full of the day's necessities and close the door without being detected. My mother will figure out that I'm gone soon enough.

Something is in the air, not a smell per se, but something that propels me to skip the bus stop and just keep walking. I don't bother with school, I know that I have bigger things ahead of me. I need to just keep moving, taking in the air, exhaling my carbon dioxide to feed the trees that line either side of our suburban house. Not real trees, mind you, little trees as old as the houses, barely a decade unto themselves. But feeling like I'm doing my part to push them along, give them a helping hand. Make sure that they don't end up as the paper towels my mother would, at this point, be mopping up coffee with, and throwing into the already shocking amount of garbage our family seems to produce.

MAN: An environmentalist?

NELLY: Just trying to avoid environmental calamity. The planet's a ticking time bomb.

MAN: I've been fighting for a recycling bin.

NELLY: Well that's great.

MAN: Hey, I'm just doing my part.

NELLY: Picture a sky on the most perfect day imaginable. Clouds are a distant memory and your body is loaded with vitamin D. SPF-40 days, sunglasses days. Imagine the bluest of blue skies. Wonderfully familiar, reminiscent of childhood sandcastles at the beach or lemonade stands or something equally wholesome. Imagine that blue – is there a name for it? Sky blue? Topaz? Cerulean? The bluest of blue-eyed blues. But someone else looks up and comments on its beautiful emerald colour. Emerald, you think. Not emerald, not even close. Not even seafoam, not even teal. But everyone's in agreement that the sky is green. Always green. Blue? They say, "How blue?" Green. And all at once one of the only givens that you know (that the sky is blue) comes into question, and you think, "How can that be?" I must be wrong – surely everyone else can't all be wrong. Blue! And it's then that you realize that they are. Everyone else has no idea. You're on your own, a different planet and you have no choice but to bask in that blue. And you bask and bask because what have you got left? Because it's you versus the world.

MAN: Is that how you feel? You versus the world?

NELLY doesn't respond.

MAN: The sky is blue.

NELLY: It was metaphorical.

MAN: What does this have to do with the coffee?

NELLY: I'm sorry?

MAN: The coffee. The coffee was spilling all over the counter and ...

NELLY: I was walking.

MAN: You were walking.

NELLY: I'm walking ... Springtime smells foul. It's supposed to be the time of year that we feel inspired, spring cleaning and rebirth and all of that, but it's also the time of year when snow banks disappear and reveal all of the secrets we hid in them over the winter. That's all I can smell as I walk.

MAN: The season.

NELLY: Yeah.

MAN: And where were you headed?

NELLY: I didn't know then.

MAN: But you know now?

NELLY: I think so. Yes.

MAN: And?

NELLY: As I continue through the labyrinth of suburbia, my weight shifts from one foot to the next. The absence of wind in my hair, though small bursts of it as I pass the clearings between each home. It's there standing on the horizon – it takes up my entire view. The elephant in the landscape that nobody wants to talk about. I'm halfway to the food court before I'm even aware I've entered it.

MAN: The mall?

NELLY: The mall.

MAN: Were you shopping?

NELLY: Not exactly.

MAN: Then what?

NELLY: They nearly butchered a kid there, you know.

MAN: Who did?

NELLY: A whole group of them.

MAN: And you saw this?

NELLY: I didn't see it exactly, I was a floor up and when I glanced over the railing, all I could see was frantic movement. And security got called. Not that that really means anything because they get called for whatever, whenever anything happens, really. But this time it seemed a bit more serious. The cops arrived too.

MAN: The cops?

NELLY: Yeah, the pigs ...

> *NELLY checks in with **MAN** for a response. None comes.*

NELLY: The real guys. The officers, not just the rent-a-cops, cuz it's not like they're a threat. And that's when I left. Not because I'd done anything wrong, but because I just didn't want to be involved. Or at least be perceived to be involved, you know, "Perception rules over intent," according to the gospel of my father. No, I left because, you know, what if they wanted witnesses? Not that I was even a witness because all I saw was a group of people all gathered around this kid. A lot of pushing and pulling, I don't know. But I could tell that something wasn't right. You know, like a gut instinct. So maybe it's not fair to say that the kid was getting butchered but sometimes you can imagine the way things play out and just feel confident that that's the reality.

MAN: So you're confident that you know the reality?

NELLY: Yeah. Well, I don't know.

MAN: If you don't know why are you spending so much time telling me about it?

NELLY: Look, I don't know what it was about, so it's best if I don't say anything about it. Because then they'll want to know more and they'll have to take down my information in case they want to contact me.

MAN: Is that what they do?

NELLY: They have some notebook where they write these things down – just the basics, name, address, gender. Which seems easy enough, probably, you know, by the book, just the basics that don't really even require any thought, but then they'd get this look of panic on their face as they'd try to assess, you know: boy, girl, boy, girl.

MAN: Why "girl"? You don't look like a ... I mean to say ... Sure, there are aspects of your appearance that ...

NELLY: Sweatsuits aren't exactly feminine, are they?

MAN: So this is a far cry from your normal attire?

NELLY: It's not exactly my taste.

    Beat.

NELLY: It would create this awkward silence between us. They'd be unsure of what to say and I'd just keep my mouth shut for the time being, right? I guess just to watch them squirm.

MAN: You like to make people squirm? Maybe people who have some power over you?

NELLY: I don't understand your question.

MAN: I think you do.

NELLY: I can't answer your questions when they're that leading.

MAN: I wouldn't ask such leading questions if you stuck to the story. You're a bit all over the map.

NELLY: Not everything's as perfectly shaped as beginning, middle, end.

Finally they'd give up and ask me for ID which normally I wouldn't even have on me because I don't carry it around. So then they'd get suspicious and it'd look like I'm involved somehow. And I don't want that. So I just avoided the whole thing and took off as soon as I saw the pigs.

MAN: If you left, then what does it matter?

NELLY: I can't tell you. But it does.

MAN: Can't tell me because you don't know?

NELLY: Because it will jade your opinion of my story if I tell you now.

MAN: And that's how it is? You decide what falls into place when?

Beat. NELLY nods.

NELLY: Never kiss and tell. Never tell anything. Don't open up. Don't speak the truth. Don't speak your mind. Don't reveal anything. Don't believe in anything. Fear others. Fear yourself. Don't challenge the world.

MAN: I'm sorry?

NELLY: My father's ten commandments.

Lighting change. MAN transforms into FATHER.

FATHER: Nelson! Nelson! Nelsooooonnn!

NELLY: What?

FATHER: Have a seat.

NELLY: Why?

FATHER: Just ... sit. Please?

NELLY does. Pause. Nothing.

FATHER: I just wanted to make sure that ...

NELLY: Dad, stop.

FATHER: That you felt like you'd thought about ...

NELLY: Dad, stop.

FATHER: About all the things we'd discussed ...

NELLY: Dad, stop it.

FATHER: Because you gave me your argument and I listened ...

NELLY: Stop, Dad.

FATHER: And I think I made myself pretty clear ...

NELLY: Dad.

FATHER: And wanted to know if you'd come to any decisions you wanted to talk about.

NELLY: No. None that I want to talk about.

Lights change. MAN returns to his normal state.

NELLY: It's like watching your life through a telescopic lens.

MAN: Meaning?

NELLY: Out-of-body experiences. That's what they're called.

MAN: I'm not following the connection.

NELLY: For my fourteenth birthday my mom bought me a telescope science kit. I'd never previously shown interest in science nor stars, nor planets, but she seemed to think it would be valuable for my development. Watching something way out there, galaxies far, far away, and all of that. Watching possibilities outside of here. Staring out into the night, full of hope of something else.

MAN: Like?

NELLY: Like something bigger than me and my family – bigger than surprise birthday gifts.

MAN: So the gift worked, then? You ended up being quite interested in the end.

NELLY: From the perspective of staring out at the world in a disjointed way that makes my importance seem insignificant, out of body, beyond me: sure.

MAN: So just walk me through this. You wake up.

NELLY: Yes.

MAN: There's coffee everywhere. You ignore it.

NELLY: Yes.

MAN: You grab your backpack, start walking to the mall. You make it there, see something that may or may not be anything, and then you take off? That's your story?

NELLY: No. There's more.

MAN: I would imagine there is, but right now it's already so scattered that it's hard to track.

NELLY: You're not taking notes? Things are easier on paper.

MAN: I'll do my job, if you don't mind.

NELLY: My father ...

MAN: That's the third time you've mentioned him.

NELLY: Is it?

MAN: I think you know that it is.

NELLY: I wasn't counting.

MAN: You're more impeccably detailed than you lead on, if you ask me.

NELLY: I didn't necessarily ask you.

MAN: Smartass. Your father?

NELLY: You want me to continue?

MAN: Why wouldn't I?

NELLY: You seem to like interrupting.

MAN: If I don't keep you on track we'll never get out of here.

NELLY: So nobody leaves till I'm done my story? Till it's all out in the open.

MAN: Something like that.

> *NELLY considers this.*

NELLY: Good.

My father and I had gotten into a "disagreement" the previous night. A fight, I usually call it, but my mom, bless her heart, insists on calling them "disagreements" because "fights" sounds so physical and violent, neither of which my family is, neither violent nor physical, in any capacity. We don't hug, which is probably a warning sign to anyone who's ever taken any psychology class because it just means we're destined for something, but, alas, in our hands-off, non-physical way, my dad and I had been fighting, the end result being the silent treatment.

> *NELLY pauses for a moment. And another moment.*

> *NELLY watches MAN intently.*

NELLY: Nothing to add?

MAN: Looking to fill every silence that comes about?

> *Another pause.*

NELLY: It was an active decision: he decided he didn't want to talk to me. Just like that. That's exactly how he said it. "I don't want to speak to you today." Which was fine by me because I didn't care one way or another. It gave me ample reason for an early escape. You've got to understand where he's coming from. He's an accountant. Or bookkeeper. Or lawyer. Or CEO.

MAN: You don't know what he does?

NELLY: I thought you weren't interrupting anymore.

MAN: No, I said I was going to keep you on track.

NELLY: I'm on track.

MAN: Your details are hazy.

NELLY: Not when they count. This is all peripheral.

MAN: Really? You don't think what your father does matters?

NELLY: I think that's a longer answer than what you're intending, don't you?

MAN: Accountant or lawyer ... it's a big difference.

NELLY: Oh, I don't know. Something with suits and paperwork with a Blackberry to feel important and a dry-cleaning bill. I'm sure you can handwash a blazer, but who am I to argue? He's a man of some importance ... mediocre importance, importance to himself, and I guess that's the only person that matters in the end, right, oneself. If we don't impress ourselves to a certain extent, then who's left?

MAN: Does the mall represent your father? You're on a quest to seek a relationship with your father by heading to the mall?

NELLY: I never said "quest." I would never use the word "quest."

MAN: You know what I'm saying.

NELLY: For someone so concerned with details, you sure do give yourself freedom. And why are you trying to psychoanalyze me? I thought you wanted my story.

MAN: But right now your story doesn't make much sense, does it? The mall and telescopes, there's no connection there.

NELLY: That you can see. Doesn't mean there isn't one.

MAN: I don't have time to play games with you.

NELLY: I thought you said nobody leaves until I'm done.

MAN: Keep on track. Just the facts.

NELLY: What else would I be giving you?

MAN goes to reply, but stops.

NELLY: Silent treatment's okay. We don't speak much anyway. Not physical, and not terribly vocal, he and I. (*resuming the narrative*) I keep walking.

MAN: Toward the mall?

NELLY: Purposeful, each step feeling incredibly freeing.

MAN: It's just walking.

NELLY: To you.

MAN: And what is it to you?

NELLY: It's a political act.

MAN: Political?

NELLY: Not everyone can be wherever they want whenever they want. Not everyone has that privilege.

MAN: Like highways?

NELLY: You don't get it.

MAN: I might if you gave me something to buy into.

NELLY: Simple, small things can make big impacts.

MAN: Yes, sure they can, but …

NELLY: I just mean that sometimes little actions matter more than you think.

I've always dreamed of having days when I had no commitments and could wander as I pleased and this had become one of them, by default. A mental health day, to recover from my over-everything father (over-important, overbearing, over-the-top) who had so tried to put a damper on me, the way things are sometimes able to hit people at the core. My father, though perhaps not a multifaceted person, has always had that secret talent.

MAN: Daddy issues.

NELLY: What kind of therapist are you?

MAN: I never said I was a therapist.

NELLY: Then what are you?

MAN: You had your chance to ask questions, but we've moved on.

NELLY: Way to exert your authority.

MAN: Easy on the tone.

NELLY: My tone sounds the way it sounds. Take it or leave it.

MAN: If only life were that simple.

NELLY: I don't think life is, but rather just some people.

MAN gets in NELLY's face.

MAN: Don't assume someone's out there watching out for you, kid. It could just be me and you. So I wouldn't get too worked up.

NELLY looks out, considers this.

MAN: So you're walking. Toward the mall. Which may be your subconscious version of your father. But where does all of this lead us? Beginning to end. All of it, yes. But where are you leading me?

NELLY: At a certain point in my life, I felt the urge to disappear. It hit me quite suddenly. Not completely unexpectedly. It seemed to me my family had been hoping for it for years. Not intentionally, mind you, but deep down, in some subconscious realm, they'd all felt that their lives would be easier without me. Can't blame them really. And so I did. One day, I vanished.

Lights change. MAN transforms into FATHER.

FATHER: Nelson! Nelson! Neeeellllssssooooon!

NELLY: I'm here.

FATHER: Oh. I didn't see you.

NELLY: Really?

FATHER: You're just so all over the place.

NELLY: You just wanted to yell.

FATHER: I never want to yell.

NELLY: But you do it often.

FATHER: No I don't. You love to exaggerate.

NELLY: You think so?

FATHER: You can blow some things out of proportion, is all I mean.

NELLY: Don't you?

FATHER: I just try to ensure that you hear what I'm saying.

NELLY: And do I?

FATHER: I'm never really sure.

NELLY: What do you want?

FATHER: What do I ... Can I not just have a little talk with my son?

NELLY: I don't know. Do you have a son?

FATHER: Nelson ...

NELLY: Please don't call me that.

FATHER: How can I not call you your name? What do I call you then? This is all terribly confusing.

NELLY: You're smart, Dad. I'm sure you can handle it.

FATHER: Why do you get so hostile so quickly?

NELLY: What did you want to talk about?

FATHER: A lot of things.

NELLY: Like?

FATHER: What you're wearing. Tomorrow. I want to talk about what you're wearing.

> *Lights change.* **MAN** *reverts back to himself. Back in the room.*

MAN: So you disappeared? You vanished.

NELLY: I'm not finished my story.

MAN: You get very dramatic.

NELLY: Maybe from an outside eye it's dramatic. Inside it's not. It's quite honest.

MAN: The theatrics of it. Even in the language you use. "Butchered"?

NELLY: I speak the way I speak.

MAN: But is that really you? Or are you trying to impress me to give the story credibility.

NELLY: I'm not making anything up, if that's what you mean.

MAN: You're beginning to sound awfully suspicious.

NELLY: Am I? I didn't think I was being interrogated.

MAN: You assume a lot of things you shouldn't.

NELLY: So do you.

MAN: You're awfully precocious.

NELLY: Chatty two-year-olds are precocious, I don't think that's the word.

MAN: What do I have to say to get you onside?

NELLY: You're not a good lawyer if you can't figure that out.

MAN: I never said I was a lawyer. Now can we stick to your story, please?

NELLY: I'm trying, but ...

MAN: I'll just need clarification every now and then.

NELLY: Your version of clarification reeks of accusation.

MAN: If you were being accused of something, you'd know.

NELLY: Right, and I should just trust that.

MAN: What you should do is make sure your sequence of events falls into place.

NELLY: I don't feel comfortable telling you the next part.

MAN: And why is that?

NELLY: It's personal.

MAN: It's all personal, it's your story.

NELLY: But ...

> MAN *becomes the authoritarian.*

MAN: Beginning to end. You've been meandering through the middle, but you have to get to the end.

Beat.

NELLY: I try to avoid mirrors. Sometimes. I avoid them when I'm naked. It just gets confusing.

MAN: How so?

NELLY: What exactly is happening down there is of no interest.

MAN: Just to clarify, you mean ...

NELLY: Yes.

MAN: Your p–

NELLY: Don't say it.

MAN: Okay.

NELLY: Just catching sight of it in the mirror ... Well. It's like staring at a car crash. You have no choice but to succumb. I'd love to avoid it. At all cost. I would. But I get easily hypnotized.

MAN: I'm not sure what to say now.

NELLY: Have I weirded you out?

MAN: I just want to be sensitive.

NELLY: Sensitivity is overrated. What are you really thinking?

MAN: I don't quite get it.

NELLY: What is there to get?

MAN: That's an odd relationship to have to your –

NELLY: Don't …

MAN: Body.

NELLY: Not all of it. Just a piece.

MAN: A piece?

NELLY: It's a bit of flesh sewn on by mistake, I think.

MAN *turns away from* NELLY.

MAN: Oh.

NELLY: I've scared you off.

MAN: You haven't, no.

NELLY: Then what?

MAN: It's a bit outside of my frame of reference.

NELLY: I shouldn't have …

MAN: Yes, you should. Just … But I'm going to ask you some questions that will … I want you to … Is it that you don't think you're male? Were you, um, what, born into the wrong body or …

NELLY: It's not as simple as having an operation if that's what you mean. Because what would I replace it with? What's the after to the before? Why is so much focus placed on what's between our legs? There's so much that people's biologies have in common, why does that get our focus?

MAN: It's a distinct separation between two things.

NELLY: But what about ears, or feet, or eyebrows, or wrists, or nipples? Who would even think we'd all have nipples? But we do! Why can't we focus on that – on the obvious.

MAN: We do. Our reflections are just that: the obvious. Both the similarities and the differences. What do you see when you look in the mirror?

NELLY: I'm sorry?

MAN: What's the reflection looking back?

NELLY: That's not what I was talking about.

MAN: Humour me.

>   MAN *gets up and looks at his reflection*
>   *in the implied observation glass.*

MAN: When I look in the mirror, I see an inherently male form. Broad shoulders, a prominent nose, flat chest, an Adam's apple. These are male attributes. But what do you see?

>   *NELLY reluctantly joins him.*

NELLY: Eyes. Kneecaps. Ribs. Toenails. Cheekbones. A bum. Things we have. We all have.

MAN: What else?

NELLY: Something else.

MAN: But what?

NELLY: Just that. I see something else. Something other than what you'd expect. I see a third.

MAN: A third what?

NELLY: Something other than male or female.

MAN: Other how?

NELLY: Other because you wouldn't be able to recognize it. You wouldn't understand it because it would compromise a duality that you thrive on. That society thrives on.

MAN: Big statements.

NELLY: In the bathroom is when I first lay eyes on it.

MAN: The bathroom?

NELLY: Yes. I'm in the bathroom. Food-court bathroom. And from there it's a downward spiral. I wouldn't say that I live a life of illusion, or even that I'm easily convinced about many things but this ... Seeing it is a shattering of reality.

MAN: What do you mean?

NELLY: It's like telling your kid that Santa doesn't exist.

MAN: But I don't understand. I mean, how could you possibly not know that –

NELLY: There are things we know intellectually, and things we know psychologically. You should know that.

MAN: Because you think I'm a therapist, right? Or a lawyer?

NELLY: Because everyone knows that. There are different ways of understanding things.

MAN: You seem awfully self-aware for someone in crisis.

NELLY: Whoever said I was in crisis?

MAN: Well then why are you here?

NELLY: Your guess is as good as mine.

> Beat.

MAN: Tell me more about this. I'm curious.

NELLY: Why?

MAN: I want to get it.

NELLY: What *it*?

MAN: You.

NELLY: I'm not as simple as a one-question response.

MAN: A third. What do you mean?

NELLY: In India they've got a third sex. Once highly respected. Not nowadays. Nowadays they're nothing. Lowest possible place in the social strata. But despite that, they still have a third option when filling out paperwork: male, female, or hijra. Hijra. Sounds beautiful, doesn't it? Here people would probably call them eunuchs.

MAN: Aren't those men who ...

> MAN *makes a snipping gesture.*

NELLY: That's not funny.

MAN: I'm not trying to be. Aren't they?

NELLY: That's a North American understanding.

MAN: Ah, but you're a worldly traveller? Are you well versed in Indian culture?

NELLY: I haven't lived in an ashram if that's what you're asking.

MAN: Is that what I'm asking?

NELLY: Is that a question? Or are you just answering with a question so you can feel like this interrogation's going well?

MAN: You still think this is an interrogation?

NELLY: I don't think I'm here for the good of my health, no. And you've made it clear that I can't leave. So I don't think I'm going out on a limb in that assumption.

MAN: Everything's more complicated than it seems with you, isn't it?

NELLY: Not just with me, I'd venture to say the world is rather complicated. Life is complicated, in fact. Not everything just falls into place, and you can't always get what you want. So sure, yes. I'm complicated.

MAN: Why are you getting angry?

NELLY: Why aren't you listening?

MAN: I'm listening, but I'm also doing my job.

NELLY: Oh really? And how's that?

MAN: I ask questions, you answer them. You veer off course, I bring you back.

NELLY: You make it all sound so simple.

MAN: It is, if you think about it. So you going to continue or what?

NELLY: I'd rather speak with someone else who listens and doesn't just question and cross-examine every step of the way. Shouldn't I have a lawyer?

MAN: One minute you think I'm your lawyer, now you're ensuring your rights are being respected. But we're just having a conversation. Do you feel you need a lawyer? Did you do something wrong?

NELLY: I think the world thinks most things I do are wrong.

MAN: Listen, kid, we can't just keep with the dramatics all day. At a certain point, you need to level with me. It's not a matter of you versus the world. It's just a story.

NELLY: That's where you're wrong. It's not just a story. It's my story. And if it's so flimsy and dispensable then why do you care? And don't call me kid. It's condescending. Like "ma'am" or "buddy." Nobody's doubting who holds the power here.

> *MAN goes to speak, but reconsiders.*
> *They sit in silence for a moment.*

NELLY: It feels like it's someone else's. Like I don't quite understand it. And I ignore it as much as I can ... But there. In that bathroom. That wasn't possible.

> *Lights change. MAN transforms into FATHER.*

NELLY: Frankly I think I'm old enough to be able to dress myself. Ultimately, it's my body and my decision, right? If my body is my temple, then I can decide how to adorn it.

FATHER: Temple?

NELLY: Fine, I don't know if my body is a temple or what, but at the very least it houses me. And therefore, I can choose how I want my walls, my exterior, my shell, if you will, to be received, and perceived, and believed.

FATHER: Listen, I'm not asking you to ... We can't always get everything we want all the time, can we? It's simply not possible, but ... I ... I just want you to think about things.

NELLY: About what I'm wearing? About how I'll look? It's not any different than the close attention you pay to your tie selection every morning.

FATHER: How do you mean?

NELLY: Well, that all depends on who you'll be negotiating with on any given day, right? It's all in the name of presentation.

FATHER: Well, I'd argue there's more to it than that.

NELLY: What, Dad? What's so different about your clothing in a meeting compared to my clothing in life?

FATHER: Are you saying that my meetings aren't real? I don't make it up, Nelson. I don't have pretend meetings when I go to the office, it's not pretend meetings that are paying for dinner and an allowance, which, I might add, I don't really have to give you. Come on, is this really even about my tie?

NELLY: It's about being real, Dad. Who's more real?

FATHER: Who's more real? What does that even mean?

NELLY: It means that you need to open your eyes and look at me before you start telling me what I need to do ...

Lights change. Return to the room.

NELLY: Swerving through excitable young couples and baby strollers. A lineup at La Senza of preteens determined their chests need support. I watch them for a minute, then keep walking. I don't want to be that creep who stares at young girls.

MAN: Surely no younger than you are.

NELLY: Staring's still staring. I sneak past the Apple Store where kids are blowing their allowances on the next model of something they already have, and I keep pushing forward. And it's important. It's vital. Life and death.

MAN: Life and death.

NELLY: Yes. Just because I'm fifteen doesn't mean my life isn't important. It's not like life starts carrying meaning when you hit forty. (*looking at MAN*) Fifty?

MAN: Easy.

NELLY: Life and death.

MAN: You can talk your way out of anything, can't you? It's no wonder that you and your father don't have a better relationship.

Pause.

MAN: I'm sorry. I didn't mean ...

NELLY: It's always the kid's fault, isn't it?

MAN: You don't speak like much of a kid.

NELLY: Sure.

MAN: I'm sorry. I am. That was out of line.

NELLY: I want to talk to someone else.

MAN: Why?

NELLY: Because you don't care about what I'm saying. You don't want to. You just go through your list of questions without any regard for what comes out of my mouth. It's formulaic for you, all of this. Just routine. But you can't just check off a box and feel you have me nailed down, can you?

MAN: I'm sorry. I am, but can you ...

NELLY: Continue? Why bother? You're not going to believe me anyway.

MAN: But we need the end of the story.

NELLY: Or what? You'll never get to leave?

MAN: Something like that.

NELLY: Who cares?

NELLY looks out through the implied mirror.

NELLY: Are you out there? Huh? I want to talk to someone else. Now!

Nothing changes.

NELLY: (*screaming*) Someone else. Right now.

MAN watches NELLY.

NELLY: And bring more water.

NELLY touches their throat.

NELLY: Is there ...

MAN: Maybe they're not listening.

NELLY: Maybe.

MAN: Just you and me then. And I'd like to hear the ending.

MAN faces NELLY.

MAN: Please, Nelly.

NELLY stares at him for a time. It's the first time MAN has said their name.

NELLY: What do you think of me?

MAN: Think of you?

NELLY: What's your impression? Your assessment?

MAN: I think you're incredibly alone.

NELLY: You don't seem like a social beacon yourself. Besides, there's a difference between being lonely and being alone.

MAN: And which are you?

NELLY: What else?

MAN: What else what?

NELLY: What else do you see?

MAN: I see something ... else. Something different than what I'd expect.

NELLY: You're mocking me.

MAN: Do you think so?

NELLY: I don't know. You're impossible to read.

MAN: Then I'm probably doing my job.

> *Beat.*

NELLY: I'm not lonely.

The mall has underground parking. For those who are still afraid of seasons. Though, like everything, even the seasons' time is coming to an end. Nothing lasts forever. It can't. It shouldn't. We'd never exist if it did. People worry about global warming, about epidemics and pandemics and carcinogens, but all of those things are maybe just telling us that our chapter's over. And that's not a bad thing.

MAN: Isn't it?

NELLY: Who are we to say that because we're at the top of the food chain, there's nothing else beyond us that should be inhabiting the planet, you know? It's been a good ride, but we can't always continue to exist. We need to share the wealth a bit.

MAN: That's certainly a conversation starter.

NELLY: People think, well, my mom used to be really concerned about that, that line of thinking. She figured it meant I was suicidal. Or at least pessimistic.

MAN: And you disagree?

NELLY: Yeah. I do. I'm neither. I'm a realist.

MAN: I still think precocious applies. Now, you've brought me this far ...

NELLY: In the underground parking, amid row after row of identical minivans, I make my way out of myself and the suburban landscape. I swerve behind a parked car, avoiding the wandering eyes of happy families. Though in all likelihood their eyes are wandering away from me. The pecked-at remnants of some Oedipal spin-off.

MAN: Pardon?

NELLY: Oedipus.

MAN: I know Oedipus, I'm just not following your imagery.

NELLY: I promise it'll make sense in the end.

MAN: Wait. Stop. I thought you were telling this in order ...

NELLY: The way I remember it, yes. I have to save the best for last, don't I?

MAN: Or you could give me a chronological play-by-play.

NELLY: But that's predictable.

MAN: Maybe, but it's also practical.

NELLY: There's your trouble. I never said I was a practical person.

MAN: So when are we now? When in the sequence of events have we arrived? You're on your way out and something's happened. What are you hiding?

NELLY: Adults assume all of us are hiding something. Like because you have so many deep dark secrets, we must too.

MAN: You're avoiding something. It's not the mall that's "the elephant in the landscape," Nelly. You and I both know that.

NELLY: What do you want?

MAN: Well, for starters, "pecked-at"? Why?

NELLY: Because of the mall.

MAN: I know, Nelly, but you need to give me more than that. I can't help you if you don't give me more.

NELLY: At the mall ... My family is gathered outside the Walmart Portrait Studio. My mom, bless her heart, thinks it's so great having a Walmart in the mall because then we never have to leave in order to find everything we could ever need. Like this is the embodiment of innovation. So we gather outside there, my mother in some kind of summery getup and my dad with a carefully chosen tie, and his usual suit. Katie, my sister, is wearing what I remember as her semi-formal dress and Katrina, her twin, in Katie's semi-formal dress from last year (she would have worn her own, but during her desperate-to-be-political phase, she focused all of her energy on hating the very idea of semi and never got one). Dad had picked the twins up from their school, but as I hadn't bothered with school that day, unbeknownst, I told them I'd just meet them at the mall. Walking all day beats the bus.

MAN: But isn't the bus more efficient?

NELLY: Sure, but when I'm walking I don't have to deal with people. I mean, I still see them, I pass them, but I don't have to acknowledge them.

MAN: And the bus?

NELLY: On the bus they're everywhere. And you can't get away. They're all around you and you don't know what might happen.

MAN: What are you alluding to?

NELLY: Nothing.

MAN: You're sure?

NELLY: It's dangerous to have too many people in confined space. The mob mentality could kick in at any moment.

> MAN *considers this.*

NELLY: Earlier I was staring at those boys in the food court, sitting not far from the bathroom, and I could tell that they'd put a lot of thought into what they were wearing. Not necessarily effort, but they certainly have thought about what their clothing said about them. Like, "Oh, my big pants and my skater shoes, I'm such a boy." Like this subversive commentary about their gender, subconscious as it may be.

MAN: Those are big words.

NELLY: No they're not. Older people just seem to think that because I'm under twenty I shouldn't have a decent vocabulary. Why do people think they send their kids to school?

MAN: People keep losing faith in public schooling, maybe because their kids don't have the vocabulary you do. Your parents should be proud.

NELLY: Should.

MAN: Have I hit a nerve?

NELLY: What do you want? For me to start bawling about the injustice of my parents and their attitude toward me? Sorry, that's not my kind of story.

MAN: I want to understand what's going on from your point of view.

NELLY: What do you mean by that?

MAN: Your sequence of events.

NELLY: Are you going to be comparing them to something?

MAN: There are always at least two sides to any issue.

NELLY: And what's the issue here?

MAN: Why don't we stick to the story?

NELLY: You asked me how to get me onside? Trust what I'm saying.

MAN: I'm doing my best.

> NELLY *crumples the empty water cup and drops it.*

MAN: Do you have a boyfriend?

NELLY: That's a personal question. And a bit misguided.

MAN: Girlfriend? Help me out here. I'm trying.

NELLY: Gender doesn't equate sexuality. Is that really a hard concept to grasp?

MAN: So you're not attracted to the skater boys, then? Eating at A&W, so masculine. Or maybe it's the La Senza girls?

NELLY: Oh, you are listening. Good. Better than I'd thought. But no, not quite. I'm not just another boy in a dress. It's like you can hear me, hear a series of words come out of my mouth, but you can't quite string them together to make any sense out of them. There's a big difference between listening and hearing.

MAN: Listening versus hearing, alone versus lonely: very binary for someone who rejects the ideas of male and female.

NELLY: I don't reject them. I just don't think they're the only options.

MAN: Aren't you afraid?

NELLY: Of what?

MAN: Of being so far on the outside.

NELLY: It's where I thrive.

MAN: Fifteen and invincible.

NELLY: Can I continue? Or are we going to harp on this ...

MAN: Will it fall into place later? The way you promise
everything will ...

NELLY: With those boys in the food court, sitting there eating
their A&W, that was the first thing I noticed, you know? Not the food,
but their existence as boys. I didn't even control it. It was completely
instinctual to want to identify that. Because, you know, without a gender,
we don't know what to do because it toys with one of the absolutes that
we believe. That some people believe. That I can't believe.

MAN: So we're back here now. With gender.

NELLY: Yes.

MAN: You don't believe in it?

NELLY: It's a conditioned concept.

MAN: How do you figure?

NELLY: Well why does everything have to be so black and white?
What happens when you're a shade somewhere in between?

MAN: Does this have to do with the bathroom? The mirror.
Your penis –

NELLY: Don't say the word. Please.

MAN: Okay, but I need answers.

NELLY: I thought we'd moved past that.

MAN: You said we'd get back to it.

NELLY gets more worked up.

NELLY: So that it can be my fault in the end, right? So that I can have some kind of mental breakdown? So you can prove to someone that I'm a freak, maybe? Hypothesize about my inability to accept that flap of skin between my legs as my own? I don't ... I don't feel male. Or female for that matter. Maybe I don't know. Maybe I'm trying to test the waters. I'm sorry, but I don't like being put in situations where I'll be forced to choose. My life is not a public-bathroom decision.

Pause.

MAN: Nelly?

NELLY: What?

MAN: I'm sorry if ...

NELLY: No.

MAN: I didn't mean that ...

NELLY: Sure.

MAN: So what happens now?

NELLY: You haven't figured it out? What kind of a detective are you?

MAN: I never said I was a detective. If you focused your energy into telling your story rather than guessing what I do, I probably could have been tucking my kids in by now.

NELLY is taken aback.

NELLY: You have kids?

MAN: Yes.

NELLY: How old?

MAN: I don't think that information's going to help you get your story out faster.

NELLY: I think it might.

MAN: They're thirteen. Twins.

NELLY: Oh.

MAN: Does that matter?

NELLY: Yeah.

MAN: How?

NELLY: Isn't it obvious?

MAN: I'm figuring out that very little about you is obvious.

NELLY: Big lesson. Unusual, having twins. Fortuitous. Another big word.

MAN: Not really. Not nowadays. In vitro – doubles the odds, doubles the results.

NELLY: Test-tube babies.

MAN: We don't like to think of it that way.

NELLY: Perfect parallel lives, and lines. Two of a kind. In agreement. Balanced.

MAN: Can't be easy living in the shadow of twins.

NELLY: It has its days.

MAN: But you seem pretty unique yourself.

NELLY: Do I?

MAN: I'd say so.

MAN smirks.

NELLY: I end up changing in the family washroom because there's privacy there and it saves the whole "Which door's safer?" routine that I'm always going through at school, and I take the time to really, you know, get ready with daddy-o's haunting "If we're going to do the photo, we're going to do it right" at the back of my mind, thinking: "Dad, why do you speak in colloquial catchphrases?" Wishing he'd at least pick up on my use of alliteration.

So I meet them, freshly changed in the bowels of the mall bathroom and as soon as they see me I hardly even have reaction time. I can just see it in their eyes immediately, this twinge of disbelief that they don't know if they should let out or repress. It stifles the "Hi" I'm attempting to get out and I end up just standing there.

Dad looks at Mom as Katie and Katrina share one of their looks that they always share whenever they don't approve of something, which is all the time. And everyone's silent, just for a moment. And it's so clear what all of this is about. Because Dad had actually sat me down the previous night in order to make sure that I wouldn't cause a "scene."

Lights change. MAN becomes FATHER.

FATHER: Go with your gut, but in doing so, respect your elders. That's me and your mother. And your grandparents. But they're not here, so that's a moot point. So think before you speak. Is that clear?

NELLY: Yeah, sure Dad, practically layman's terms.

FATHER: I'm not trying to rule your life here, I just want to clarify the dress code.

NELLY: (*to MAN*) For our family portrait. He wanted me to –

FATHER: Think carefully about how you want to look in the photo. Perception is everything, you know. It certainly rules over intent. And since we're sending these to your grandparents …

NELLY: (*to MAN*) And my aunts, all of whom are old maids, who's more real there?

FATHER: It's your choice. It is. I'll give you that. But you need to consider time and place and … Just think about us, Nelson.

NELLY: (*to FATHER*) That's not my name.

(*to MAN*) And I did. A lot. And it led me to certain decisions.

And thus I showed up … dressed to the nines. In a dress.

MAN: A dress?

NELLY: A real dress. Maybe that's what the big deal was, maybe it was that I looked far better than Katie or Katrina could ever hope to, because certainly everyone had already seen their semi-formal dresses, even the grandparents because they're always asking for pictures of the twins. But at that moment Dad finally parts his lips and out it comes. It's beyond expected at this point and I just want to know how explosive it's going to be. I'm edgy with anticipation. And his lips part further and sound comes out and I notice Katie and Katrina reacting but I'm not really hearing it; I'm sort of frozen mid-thought, on the brink of reacting, and then it lands.

FATHER: NELSON!

NELLY: There's a hand waving in my face and it's already getting attention from other patrons wandering around the mall, they're gawking as they divert their children's eyes, thinking they don't want them to grow up to be like me and so if they don't see me then maybe I don't exist. But they're so wrong – because even if it's just the very idea of me, I do exist and I want to challenge their children to look at me.

FATHER: Nelson.

NELLY: ... he says, in that firm "I'm taking control as the family patriarch and you will obey everything I say" tone.

FATHER: Nelson, you will take off that dress and put on something appropriate.

NELLY: I don't want to respond because he knows that I never answer people who address me by that name, and so until I hear the word Nelly come out of his mouth he may as well just stop. "That's not my name, Dad!" And then it's the eye-roll and I know that the war's just begun. The mothers are milling about and I can hear wisps of conversation from the expectant mothers, and the grandmothers talking about growing up in their day and how that never would have happened.

FATHER: Nelson, how dare you ...

NELLY: And those are the magic words that just make me shut right off.

Have you ever felt like you were the only person on the planet? Or at least the only person like you?

MAN: What do you mean?

NELLY: That no matter where you go, no matter how hard you try to fit in, you can't succeed, because even if no one notices you, you still feel like everyone's staring.

MAN: I don't think I have.

NELLY: You're constantly blowing people's glances and body language out of proportion because you've convinced yourself that it's about you. And it rarely is. But how do you get past that? How do you stop doing something you've spent a lifetime being convinced of? That's me. That's my daily routine.

MAN: That can't be easy.

NELLY: It's not. Maybe that's why I look exhausted. My dad always tells me that. That I look exhausted and yet it's obviously not from studying. But I can't, Dad, because my brain's so wrapped up in just getting by. Just making do.

After a moment, MAN continues.

MAN: Nelly?

NELLY: Yeah.

MAN: Can you finish the story?

NELLY: Yeah.

MAN: Are you sure?

NELLY: You wanted all of it.

MAN: I've probably heard enough.

NELLY: No ... That's the problem with the shades of grey, right? Nobody ever wants the whole story. They hear half of it and they assume the rest. Fill in the blanks for themselves. They figure if we don't suit the black or the white, then we don't need a full finished story. But this is my story and I will tell it. Beginning to end.

MAN: Go on then ...

NELLY: Dad's still talking and I'm making it clear that the conversation's over, half of me wanting to head back to the family washroom just to admire the dress in the privacy of the dirty mirror under bad neon light, but at least somewhere. Somewhere that isn't here, in this moment. I even consider sprinting through the mall, making everyone gasp at the sight of me, showing off to the A&W boys.

And then it happens. Dad's right in front of me, really close and he begins grabbing at the dress, seemingly trying to tear it off as if my nudity wouldn't be more of a scandal. Then my mother's moving and I think she's coming to my help, to calm him down, drag him off to the McDonald's beside the portrait studio just to ease his mind or something, buy him one of his beloved apple pies, but she doesn't. She won't even look me in the eyes as she joins him. Then Katie and Katrina aren't far behind.

There's other people, the gawking mothers who, no longer hiding their children's faces, but encouraging them to join in, and they're trying to tear off the ribbon around me, and then the outer layers, the sleeves, starting at the seams and continuing deeper and deeper. And it doesn't stop. They're trying to tear me apart, limb from limb. More and more of them join in, a sea of them. I'm being swarmed. I'm completely surrounded and I don't know what to say or do. And I can feel my joints and ligaments starting to separate. Hear the severing of my body. And I could swear that I'm floating out of it. I can see in my peripheral vision that mall security has shown up, and the police are arriving too, they're not far behind. The real ones, the pigs, not the rent-a-cops.

In the midst of all of this I stare up, looking in a final desperate attempt, for a way out of this, of all of this. And I see it. Standing there observing with this touch of concern, this look of not really being able to discern what's happening, but feeling some sort of compassion for the victim there, unsure of where to look, where to focus ... it's ... it's me. It's like I'm staring back through Mom's telescopic lens. And I stare into my own eyes, pleading for support. And once again it's like time is standing still. Out-of-body experience. I await some sort of response and then it seems like it's coming. And I start to see myself move my feet, a step forward, and then leaning on the railing, trying to get a good look, but not really being sure of what's being seen, and this look of panic coming over my face. I see my eyes shift to the cops and back to me, and then ... then ... I'm running away so as to not have witnessed it. And everyone is all around me, and I catch my father's eyes. And who's more real now, Dad? Who's more real? And then I'm gone.

MAN *shifts in his chair.*

NELLY: Lights in the distance. Another Breathalyzer stop. I don't even hesitate. Pigs aren't trustworthy animals. They'll eat anything. Even murder evidence. I imagine these pigs are much the same. There are two cars, both with flashing lights. But no one pulled over. And then suddenly, a glare. Flashlights in my face and I'm blinded.

The car ride to the station was at least warm.

Lights change. Back in the room.

Beat.

NELLY: Look at me. Please.

MAN: I am looking.

NELLY: Look deeper.

MAN: This is as far as I can look.

NELLY: Did you get all of it?

MAN: I think so.

NELLY: Do you believe me?

MAN: I believe what's true.

NELLY: What does that mean?

MAN: Everything has a truth buried underneath somewhere.

NELLY: Can I ask you something?

MAN: Of course.

NELLY: Have your children ever done something to make you that mad?

MAN considers this.

MAN: No. I don't think so. Nelly, I ...

NELLY: I'm sorry. I am.

MAN: What for?

NELLY: All of this.

MAN: We're all sorry. All of the time. But we can't be sorry forever. Now I've listened. And I have one last question for you.

NELLY: Already?

MAN: Do you believe everything you've said to me?

NELLY: I've never said a word I don't believe. Committing to the act of getting them out requires a sense of belief.

MAN: I'm not saying that I don't believe you.

NELLY: Aren't you?

MAN: But you embellish a bit.

NELLY: I told you my story.

MAN: Variations of it, parts of it. Clues. You paint a vivid story, but the gaps seem to outweigh the chapters.

NELLY: You're getting your metaphors mixed up.

MAN: That's not the point.

NELLY: Then what is?

MAN: You need to sort through it, Nelly. Refine your details.

NELLY: What do you mean?

MAN: That's not how the report reads.

NELLY freezes.

NELLY: What report?

MAN: Every story has at least two versions. You need to isolate yours. They'll want to hear all of it. To compare.

NELLY: Who?

MAN: The officer, Nelly.

NELLY: But you ...

MAN: He'll need all of it. Beginning to end. You can leave out the embarrassing bits. About your ... It's best not to confuse anyone, because they'll look for an out.

NELLY: What are you saying?

MAN: Tell them what they want to hear and it will all be over quickly. But stay on track. I can't hold your hand through it.

NELLY: So that's it? I get to the end and it only begins again?

MAN: I couldn't leave until you reached the end. And now I'm done.

NELLY: Who are you? Honestly.

MAN: Who do you think, Nelly?

> MAN *gets up to leave. Lights change.*
> MAN *transforms into* FATHER.

FATHER: Nelson? Are you asleep?

NELLY: Yes.

FATHER: Oh ... I just wanted to say goodnight. Before –

NELLY: I made any rash decisions. So I could subconsciously make a smart choice for tomorrow?

FATHER: Something like that, sure. Smartass.

NELLY: Goodnight.

FATHER: Goodnight ... I'll see you in the morning.

NELLY: Sure.

> *FATHER touches NELLY's face. Lights change.*
> *FATHER returns to state as MAN, who is still*
> *touching NELLY's face – their first contact.*

> *NELLY goes to speak, but MAN stops NELLY.*

MAN: Don't say anything more.

NELLY: No, you don't understand. I can't. I can't go back to that.
There's nothing left to go back to. I'm one of those people that fall in
between the cracks and disappear. And you can't prevent that. Nothing's
ever black and white. Nobody cares about the shades of grey.

> *MAN considers this.*

MAN: Go. Leave.

NELLY: What if it's not all true?

MAN: What if it is?

> *MAN opens Nelly's paper bag, revealing a fully*
> *restored dress. He lays it out on the table. A challenge.*

> *NELLY strips naked. MAN turns away.*
> *NELLY puts on the dress and adjusts*
> *it, staring at their reflection.*

> *MAN stares at NELLY and smiles.*

> *NELLY exits the room back onto the highway.*
> *We hear the sound of highway traffic. NELLY*
> *takes it in, takes in the audience, and smiles.*
> *NELLY raises his/her head and*
> *continues walking along the road.*

> *Blackout.*

MY FUNNY VALENTINE

PRODUCTION HISTORY

My Funny Valentine was commissioned by Zee Zee Theatre and developed with the Playwrights Theatre Centre's Playwrights Colony, with dramaturge Don Hannah. A workshop production was part of the 2009 SummerWorks Performance Festival. It was first produced by Zee Zee Theatre at the PAL Studio Theatre in Vancouver, British Columbia, Canada, from April 15 to 24, 2011, with the following cast and crew:

BERNARD, GLORIA, HELEN, HAL, RAY, ROGER, RHONDA, and THE COLLECTOR	Kyle Cameron

Director	Cameron Mackenzie
Set and Costume Designer	Marina Szijarto
Lighting Designer	Jergus Oprsal
Sound Designer	Shawn Sorensen
Stage Manager	Jillian Perry

PRODUCTION NOTE

My Funny Valentine is performed by a single actor portraying multiple characters. Besides the seven characters who appear onstage, there is an eighth character: **THE COLLECTOR**. He has collected materials pertaining to the case in question and sifts through them throughout the piece. Each character he embodies grows out of these materials in order to manifest onstage. **THE COLLECTOR** is the neutral state of the actor onstage, who we see between each monologue.

CHARACTERS

BERNARD, forty-two

GLORIA, fourteen

HELEN, forty-two

HAL, sixty-six

RAY, thirty-seven

ROGER, thirty-three

RHONDA, eleven

THE COLLECTOR, ageless

Kyle Cameron as Helen in Zee Zee Theatre's 2011 premiere production of
My Funny Valentine at PAL Studio Theatre.
Photo by Brandon Gaukel, courtesy of Zee Zee Theatre.

Anton Lipovetsky as Hal in Zee Zee Theatre's 2013 remount production of
My Funny Valentine at Firehall Arts Centre.
Photo by Tina Krueger Kulic, courtesy of Zee Zee Theatre.

BERNARD:

BERNARD, forty-two, sits in a hotel lobby.

My daughter Georgia grew up crazy about peaches. Something about the fuzz, the taste. The colour, maybe? She couldn't get enough. My wife thought that we'd fed her too many Gerber peaches as a babe. But little Georgia, she decided quite quickly what she did and didn't like, so what are you gonna do, say no? Starve her? No. It's exciting when young people make their own decisions.

We brought our Georgia to Georgia one year. The girl to the state. The Land of Peaches, and she's five years old by then. We arrange for her to go and pick her own right off the tree. Holding her up high on my shoulders and she's taking bites here and there and Marlene has to scold her, "Honey, we can't eat them all at once, we have to pick them first." Just gently. That's a lovely memory. Something so charmingly innocent about Georgia picking Georgia peaches, this gorgeous little babe of ours, doing her finest rendition of a Southern belle.

And it becomes this beloved family story: Georgia's Georgia peaches. I tell it for years over and over. And she can recite it from memory. And then there comes a point when it's not cool anymore. She doesn't want to hear it and she most definitely doesn't want to tell it. So what do I do? I write it down. There you go. I just don't want to let go of it. But as I'm writing it, that's when I realize that I like this. Writing. Me, of all people. It's just one of those things you fall into – you can't plan what life throws at you, but every now and again you step back and take inventory of what's in your life, what you've become versus your expectations, and, let me tell you, there are bucketloads of surprise there. So from there, I decide to try my hand at little local news stories. Not at first, at first it's more just hanging around the office watching what everyone does. It's a small paper. A free paper. Easier that way, I bet. So you get a feel for it, find what they call your writer's voice. They're idiotic stories, really, but someone out there is reading them. Prized goat, local fire department with most logged volunteer hours, a feel-good piece about a little girl's organ transplant. That one I actually didn't mind because she looked an awful lot like my daughter at that age.

Oh, and surfers. You definitely get your surfer coverage. Christ in a
bucket, this city lives for surfing. Not for me, though. I'm more of a
peaches kind of guy. So when something big happens, Christ, you're the
first in line, you're begging for it to be your story.

It sounds awful to say out loud, but when you're a journalist other
people's misfortune is your success. You trade pain for profit, in a way.
I don't mean actual profit, God, this is my first paid gig for the paper, but
I'm actually being called a reporter. Before I was, what, a hobbyist?

When the news broke, I was in a compromised position. Okay, I was
having sex with my wife. Morning sex. No, not an illicit affair, none of
that just, well, awkward role-playing at an even more awkward motel. Like
an awful place that you'd never actually stay but you figure for Valentine's
Day you'll try to spice it up, be spontaneous; it's not breakfast in bed this
year, it's out the door two hours early. Dropping Georgia off for her swim
practice and then straight to the motel check-in. All this to keep things
exciting, to pretend to be someone else, to create a sense of danger, that
beautiful something you had when you first started out together.

The TV got turned on because we were loud, because we didn't want
the neighbours to hear – not neighbours really, whoever rented the next
room who you hope, for their own sake, aren't actually staying here. And
quite honestly they're probably used to hearing next-door fornication
in a place like this, but you figure it's the nice thing, the responsible
thing to do.

It becomes this awkward dance of thrusting, thrusting, almost there, little
more … and then … little bit more … thrusting … and? And? Thrusting
and? Fucking hell. Are you close? Are you going to? Oh, me too.
Definitely me too. But not quite yet, just …

And you're turning up the volume louder and louder, that's good, it's not
that I don't want to … Thrusting. And then, SHIT. STOP!

Because there it is, on TV, and it's not that you don't want to finish, and
it's not that you don't want it all to be perfect, this mishap Valentine's
Day. Not even Valentine's Day. She has to work, so here you are two days
earlier trying to make a go of something. Just a little something.

But some things don't always work out.

There it is. On TV. Shots fired at a local high school. This is my opportunity. Someone else's misfortune.

So I rush to get dressed. And I'm in the car driving faster than I've ever driven because I just need to be there, I need this to be my story. I don't even bother calling the office because they'll give this one to someone higher up, someone more experienced. But this is mine, dammit.

It sounds awful to say it out loud, but somehow the weight of the story never landed then. It's like two separate parts of the brain and they're not talking to one another. One part registers the tragedy of murder, but the other just sees the work ahead, it's very practical, and it just needs me to get to the scene first so that I can stake my claim. And that's the only part of the brain that I have time for. I'm not even pushing the other half away, it just doesn't rank.

I write the piece. I write it in a heartbeat and send it into the office. They never assigned it to me. I was showing initiative.

Well, it paid off.

They ran that story in papers across the country. With my name, right there in the byline. "Bernard Michaels." Paired it with this photo of the kid. The kid who got shot. Wearing this tiny sweater. If I didn't know any better, I'd think that the photo was life-size. I'd think I could fit that little imp in the palm of my hand. And wouldn't you know it, I don't know if it's a particular look in his eyes, but I can hear myself murmuring something as I stare at that photo, the first time I see it in print. And it's Georgia's Georgia peaches. I'm telling my story to a little photo of a dying boy.

Because he's Georgia's age. Fifteen, now, but he looks ... He looks like he could use a good story.

So tonight ... I need to get a better hotel. Marlene said she wanted to celebrate me officially becoming a journalist, but I dunno ...

Because I keep it here, in my wallet. Weird, right? I keep that picture in here next to the photo of my daughter and my wife. It's like a little thank-you card, maybe.

And I think that's all the celebration I need.

GLORIA:

> *GLORIA, fourteen, is at school.*
> *She scribbles in a notebook.*

(*writing*) "Everything matters eventually."

Hmm.

"Everybody matters eventually."

That isn't even true.

"Everybody hates eventually."

Uh ...

"Everybody hates somebody."

God, yes. Even me. Even like those really perfect religious people who claim to love everyone. Especially them. Like they only love people because their faith guilts them into it. They're the ones to watch out for. Because, like, they never actually like you, not really. They'll say it to your face, but they're not praying for you at night, that's for sure. Not even close. Always watch out for people who don't admit their flaws. Dangerous.

I shouldn't say "hate." It's not what I mean. It's a strong word, apparently. Apparently we're only supposed to use it when we mean it. But, like, I think, who the hell is anyone to tell me what I mean? I know what I know.

(*resuming writing*) "Everything matters eventually."

It's meant as some kind of philosophical springboard to get us in the mood for creativity. I'm creative. It has nothing to do with my mood, though, you don't just turn it on and off, you either are or you aren't, and Gloria is creative. This is just meant to be something to get us fired up. So you change it. You make it yours because that statement isn't even true. Because not everything does or should matter. Not everyone either. Some people, hell, half the people in this classroom won't matter eventually. Not to me. Not to each other. My uncle says that you only take two or three people you know from high school through the rest of your life. So who the hell are the rest of them and why do I need to try to like them?

High school is like a reality TV show. *Big Brother* or something. Take all of these messed-up personalities, nothing in common with each other, oh, except that we came into the world around the same time and live remotely in the same shit town. And then you force them all into a box. And you tell them to like each other. But life's not like that. Just because I'm riding the same way as the person next to me on the bus doesn't mean we're friends, it just means that I want McDonald's and he needs to get to the bank before it closes, and if it weren't for the time crunch he'd walk. Just cuz he's near me doesn't mean I need to care.

"Everything matters eventually." Yeah, right.

I look around the room and I could forget all of these faces easily enough. And I will. They'll mean nothing to me eventually. You mark my words.

In the long run I'll do my best not to remember any of this. Not to be born into the Lima bean capital of the country. Not to have our strawberries be our pride and joy. It's a stupid claim to fame. Not to live in a town where James Cameron lives because I don't care how much money he spent on that *Avatar* movie, it still just looked like a shiny cartoon. And if I could have even one percent of that money, then I wouldn't be in this predicament right now, now would I? And he made more money than anyone on the planet this year. So him living here just creates this expectation that we're more special than any other town or city or place. But we're not New York City. So who cares?

Oh no, Gloria will block all of it. Maybe fly across the country to meet some online random and start again. Take on new friends and interests and hope for the best. But something to get out of here. Or move to New York and live with my boyfriend.

When I find a boyfriend.

New York boys would kill for a piece of this.

People can argue all they want that here isn't so bad, that we have good weather, and surfing, but I don't wear bikinis. And they say that two hundred thousand isn't really a town, it's a city. That I just complain too much. But come on, nobody likes the place they grow up. And someday, when I've hit it big doing something, someone will ask me what my high school experience was like, and I'll tell them straight up that I don't remember. It was so long ago, and unmemorable, and that everything that's happened to me since is far more interesting.

So I'm getting out. Working my ass off. Babysitting. But there are only so many hours in a week that children need supervision. But if you're determined to do something, you make it happen. You encourage parents to leave their kids in your care. I don't even like kids, but it beats drive-thru.

How else am I going to get the hell out of here? By saving up and dreaming big. People always tell kids to "dream big," and I have to think, "Yeah, look around: you don't think we are?"

So I keep babysitting, even though the kids are demons. Total demons. Rich parents make for demon spawn. But I'm determined. And my parents don't want to help me out, they want me to focus on school as if that's the solution to every one of life's problems. "Just keep working hard, honey." Right. So here I am doing it on my own, working my ass off to fill that Doritos bag full of cash. Doritos because my parents would never think to look, because they don't like cheese flavour, though they still serve Kraft macaroni and cheese to me and my sister for dinner. They eat something else. They eat the "adult" food, like steak. And then somehow the "kids," as we get called, we get stuck with the shit food. Shouldn't we have the nutrients? Aren't we the ones growing? I'll be sure to remember this when I end up remaining five foot nothing for the rest of my life. Gloria the midget.

The money's safer in the chip bag. Thieves never take snack food.

And I just about got enough to make the big move. To get the hell out of here. To forget it all.

And that's the day when the gunshot goes off.

Not in here, down the hall. But we all hear it. And people are running.
Not screaming. Not at first. First it's freaky quiet. Like, way worse than
if everyone was panicking. It's natural to scream. We should. This is
terrifying. Nothing ever happens around here. Not really.

And a second shot. And people are scattering.

And there, right then, is the moment, the moment that two of the three
people I'll take with me into life is sealed. Just like my uncle said. There
are now two names that I will never forget. That will make high school
something else. Make it all stick. That will make me have to work even
harder to push all of this away. To reinvent myself. Nothing will ever
overpower the fact that I went to a school where a kid shot another kid.
And that kid died. I will never forget those names, I'll tell you that much.

Even if I change my own name. But I like Gloria. Gloria's the
name of a star.

So isn't this all lovely. I bust my ass trying to make something and it
blows up in my face. Thanks a lot. At least it's better than Lima beans.

My parents are watching me like a hawk now. Can't even babysit. I don't
miss those asshole kids, but I miss the money. That chip bag's still got a
bit of room. So what now?

Everything matters eventually. Yup.

And I cleaned up baby puke for this.

HELEN:

> *HELEN, forty-two, enters the school gymnasium.*

Damn! Damn! Damn!

> *She's running late for her own meeting. She fumbles with her purse. It's 2008.*

I'm here! Hello! Sorry!

> *She takes a final sip of the cup of coffee she's holding and inadvertently spills it all over herself.*

Oh shit!

Ummm. Sorry. I ...

> *She finds her way to her seat.*

These new coffee machines remain a mystery. A class of thirty is no problem but give me more than one button and ... Christ, how do I manage to stain my clothing before 9 a.m.? It's a hidden talent, really. I'll just Tide-to-Go it ... I'll be fine.

> *She gets herself together. The pain sets in.*

Oh. Ouch. That is hot. Funny how you worry about the stain first, the burning flesh later. That's gonna bubble up. Did I bring the tea tree? It's probably in my other purse, shit. Oh well.

> *Pause. She dabs at the stain with a tissue.*

Okay. Now. Ahem. Sorry for my late arrival. Just one of those days, isn't it? Am I right?

Right.

Okay. Thank you all for coming. Thank you. Your being here is more important than you know. Though maybe it's not. Maybe you do know. We're all connected, one way or another. Tragedy has a way of bringing people ... Ahem.

My husband chose this outfit today. I didn't inherit the fashion gene. He's better at this kind of thing. Getting the point across. I can handle kids, no problem, it's adults I struggle with.

Did I just say that out loud? I did. Wow. Great start. Okay. Let's start again. Can we? Just try it again and this time I won't even try for that final sip. No coffee.

She stands. Exhales.

Ladies and gentlemen, concerned parents, teachers. I'm here today to ...

Well in the wake of ... Everything. I felt it important to ... Talk. About anything. Just talk. Don't you think? We shouldn't be living in our own mourning, our own fear and concern. We need to vent it all out. In the open.

But specifically ... I believe that we have the capacity to make a change.

There's been a document that ...

In 1998, when Matthew Shepard ...

There's been a lot of talk around building a document for schools to protect students, to educate them so that nothing like that would ever ... But it has. Hasn't it?

So here we are today. To talk about what that might look like. Hindsight is twenty-twenty, all of that.

Part of the role of a school is to teach young people how to function in a democracy. In a democracy, we protect the minority from the tyranny of the majority. Where else are they going to get that lesson? They've got to learn it in school. So how to phrase this? Because phrasing is vital, I believe that. If I didn't, I wouldn't be an English teacher. Someone once said, "To teach you have to love the language so much your husband gets a little jealous."

But language is something that is dear to my heart. And in keeping with that we need to be very selective. If you'll humour me for a moment, I brought my dictionary. It sounds nerdy, but there's a point.

She reaches into her bag and pulls out a travel-size, English-language dictionary.

Definition, according to the *Oxford Dictionary of English*: "To allow (something that one dislikes or disagrees with) to exist or occur without interference; to patiently endure (something unpleasant); to be capable of continued exposure to without adverse reaction." That's what it means to tolerate. And so you can see why I don't like that word. Tolerance isn't what we're striving for. We're striving for equality among our students. And not acceptance either. It comes from the same line of thinking. Submitting to a belief that we're told we must.

She returns the dictionary to her purse and discovers a bottle of tea-tree oil.

Of course, there's the tea tree. I thought I had it, but ... Why do we doubt ourselves? We're sentient human beings with rational thoughts, aren't we? Why not just trust them?

She applies tea-tree oil to her finger.

These Australian plants are just staggering, aren't they?

Umm ... Right.

She puts the tea-tree oil back in her purse.

Allow me, for a moment, if you will, ladies and gentlemen, to speak from personal experience. Because it's in the personal that we can really appreciate the bigger picture, right? It's why we watch talk shows, to get insight into other people's lives so that we can relate to the struggles they're dealing with as they pertain to our own.

We all know that kids are growing up faster than we've ever known, and not just eleven-year-olds with chests, but more than that. There are things we're not remotely covering. What I'm talking about is a serious need to educate our students; the younger the better. Because ... Let's go back five years, can we? Just for a moment, we'll pretend. Five years ago the world isn't that different for you and me. But YouTube hasn't been invented yet, so young people don't yet have the power to broadcast to millions in the blink of an eye. Broadcast, in many cases, things that aren't appropriate, but there aren't necessarily parents in the room because they can't be in the room all the time and we live in a technological age where a cellphone can pretty much access all of the information of the universe. Well, five years ago a boy came out to me. A troubled boy, some might say. He craves attention from the others. Maybe it's attention that he's not getting elsewhere and so of course he's hungry for it. This boy takes me aside as the bell rings, as everyone's heading out the classroom door. He takes me aside, and he's, what, ten years old? Isn't being ten hard enough? And he declares, in a voice I've never heard coming from a ten-year-old, a confident, announcing voice, he tells me he's gay. Just like that. At ten. And that's a tremendous risk, a huge act of courage. But that doesn't deter him. The risks attached to stating that out loud don't register for this impish little boy because he's determined not to hide behind anything.

And you don't take that lightly. You can't. It becomes a huge responsibility, you want to make sure you do right by him.

Five years goes by quickly, doesn't it?

Maybe the school simply was not equipped to have that kind of student in attendance. It doesn't matter how liberal-minded the faculty and student body are, or even how much support you have from the parents, if there isn't documentation that states quite openly that there is defence for this child, then there's no safety net.

Listen, I know that the education system isn't perfect. I've been teaching long enough to be well versed in that harsh reality. I'd be a fool if I believed it was. But I think we as educators, as parents, hell, as human beings have a responsibility to do everything in our power to ensure the safety and well-being of our students. Whether they decide to wear makeup and heels to class or not, male or female or otherwise. And so if we're going to do this, we need to do this right. This isn't a question of tolerance or acceptance. But of survival.

A student I care for deeply, passionately, who had the courage to tell me something intimate about himself, that he'd never told anyone, that student is dead. I sat at his funeral and did my best to stay calm. Just to put these things into perspective, okay? So I'm coming at this with a vested interest. More than that.

My husband Frank is a sweet, sincere man who simply doesn't get it. He tries, he does. But ... He sat me down last night to talk me out of all of this. It's not that he doesn't support the cause, not at all. He believes in human rights, in education, in equality; I wouldn't have married him if he didn't.

"You're emotional, Helen," he said.

But come on, of course I'm emotional. Have you been reading the papers? Have you? Have you seen the aftermath? It's shocking. All of it. These parents are lost and confused, they don't know what to do. No one does. And yet this is happening, more and more it seems. Columbine was supposed to prepare us for anything, wasn't it? And in those ten years, we still react the same way. Something like this happens and we panic.

The parents end up suing anyone in sight, anything they can get their hands on. The vice principal, the group home, pointing fingers any which way, but. "But." Ha! I say that a lot, don't I? "But." But what? But nothing. That's the way it is and who am I to try to do anything about it? He's said it himself, it's not my battle. And he's right. But, there's that word again, "but." But it eats away at you – it overwhelms you and consumes you until it's not an option anymore. Yes, I'm not right there in the middle of it. I know. I know. However, however, I need to try. So just let me try.

So let's do something about it, right? Let's not just light candles and pray. Not that that's not ...

What I'm saying is, the time to be proactive is now, right? So let's do it. Let's open the floor, ladies and gentlemen. I'm all ears.

I think I've said enough.

HAL:

HAL, sixty-six, sits at home in a recliner.

You click a button. It closes a window. It's that simple. It's one little X in the corner and it's gone. Just like that. It's the tiniest little action.

And I'm learning. I'm learning a whole lot more than I imagined I would want to. It's not what I grew up with. I like a typewriter. The keys have weight.

It's a learning curve, sure. Things change. You have to keep up. You have to, or you become obsolete, and I'd say I still have too many years in me to be obsolete.

I want to live them now. You know, for the years that it wasn't really living. For the years when it was just doing anything to avoid my father finding out. That was a crippling fear.

See you've got to understand that being gay was illegal then. These kids now they don't know anything about that. And I can hear that old man in me already with the "these kids" this, but it's true. It's a different world now. Now these kids worry that they'll miss the next episode of their favourite show that's got a gay kid right there in the cast. And that gay-kid character is kissing another one. On prime-time TV. That's not the same thing. That's got nothing to do with the world that I knew. There again, "the world I knew": I make it sound like I'm preparing for my own wake.

The biggest fear was being sent to prison. And they could. Doesn't sound like a threat today, does it?

Not that he didn't suspect, my father. He must have suspected. You try, you try not to look like that, to be one of them. And you keep thinking of it as a "them" because you have no real images of what a homosexual might look like. It's all pedophiles then. That's the image. It's men in sweater vests diddling little boys. It's men being coddled by their mother until they become royal fuck-ups. And that's not me, that's not going to be me, no siree. Not happening. So you do your best to blend in. To pass.

And if you try hard enough, you do. You're all alone in it. Because even if there are others around like you, they're trying even harder to pass so that you'll never find them. Feels like.

Fifteen. When I was fifteen we used to shoot pop bottles in the backyard. At first. At first I did. But then my father started to get involved and again, there's something to prove. "Pop bottles just shatter, that's not the same thing," he says. No, he brings me out to find rabbits. Except I had shit aim, so I only ever hit a rabbit once.

Have you ever looked at something while it's dying? It's enough to make you never want to go near a firearm again. I threw up. Couldn't eat for the rest of the week. Even when your mind calms down, your insides can't. It's enough to make a vegetarian pacifist out of you, I'll tell you that much.

And that comes back to me now. All of that. At fifteen ...

It's right there in the paper, February 12: fifteen and shot twice in the head in the school computer lab, and then on life support. And then brain-dead the next day, just like that. They said they were keeping him alive to remove some organs for donation. You know, so it's not a total loss. So that something can come of it. And then Valentine's Day. Now that's a day. Changes now. Not just hearts and little boys with angel wings. A death on a holiday changes the shape of that day, doesn't it?

And I have to wonder, you know, had that other kid shot something before? They say he'd been to the firing range, training, that kind of thing. But one rabbit and I think that wouldn't have happened.

For me fifteen was about proving manliness to my father and then getting the hell out of his way.

Today kids all have their own phones and computers. Even the little guys have them. These tiny things, but they know how to do it. They know how to do it better than their parents, that's the unbelievable part. You see a five-year-old being pushed by his mother in a cart at the grocery store and he's dialing daddy – he knows how. He just knows. Kids are doing their own thing.

That other kid, that kid with the gun. The kid that shot him with a gun in the middle of the computer lab? In the middle of everyone just clicking windows away, typing sweet nothings to each other. I wonder about that kid. About the look on his face when they deliver a life sentence. Does he picture what that looks like? That's what I want to know. Does he sit there picturing what his life will be at forty now. At sixty? What it might have been otherwise?

Maybe kids are getting dumber. Real-world dumber. No life smarts at all. Kids used to have them. Out of necessity. They needed to get to work, there just weren't as many options. Kids used to have to toughen up, make the kill, skin it without flinching, they used to have to cut tendons and breathe that vomit back down their throats. That's not today.

Maybe that's TV's fault. Maybe that's reality TV's fault nowadays. The only way people can think to make a life or name for themselves is by doing something insane for viewers at home, just to make a million. And I watch it too. Because you adapt. When you get older you're constantly having to adapt. See, what they don't get is teenagehood is just the practice round. You'll get older and have more things on your plate, but you're still going to have to finish them all.

Fifteen. I remember that. That's why I closed the window. One little click, just like that. Because I know what people think of old men who chat with boys. I spent my whole life avoiding that label and no one's going to point that finger now. I didn't skin a rabbit to have this happen. So you just click it closed.

He says hi. Just hi. Not "Hi, Hal." He doesn't know my name. It's just a "hello."

And there's that photo. And I think, "God, how old is this kid." Fifteen?

I click it closed. Nope. Nothing more.

I would have liked to send someone a "hello" at fifteen. Of course I would have. But it's a lot harder on a typewriter.

But if I'd said something … Nope, I can't. I can't get into the "could I have changed anything" place. Nope, nope, nope. He felt alone? Sure, maybe. I did too. That's a rite of passage. It's a shit one, but it's true. For some of us.

For some.

But good for him. Good for him for living loud. Good for that.

I've still got that gun. That pellet gun of my father's. Damned if I know why. Never used it after the rabbit. Just had to pretend. Throw out some of the ammo so that he'd think I'd been using it.

The things we do.

RAY:

RAY, thirty-seven, sits at a bar.

My boss is a fruit who lives for any bit of power he can throw in your face.

He thinks ...

He's so fucking sure of himself and that ...

Right. Yeah, right. Fucking great.

And I just want to go in there and say, "Fuck you, and fuck the horse you rode in on, you smug son of a bitch. You think you can just tell me I'm fired and that's that? Like I haven't worked my ass off and I'm not going to put up a fight? I sure as hell am, you cocksucker. I sure as hell am. No, I'm not fired. As a matter of fact, I'm going to get your damn job, you mark my words."

But then you can't say that, can you? You can't say that to some butt pirate who's weaseled his way to the top of the food chain. These gays talk about how they have such a hard time. "Equal rights" this. "Our young kids are dying" that. "Marriage." Go on ahead, get married. If it'll get you out of my face, go to it. Or here's an idea, go start up a gay fucking island, as far as I'm concerned. You can do whatever the hell you want there but you're not going to tell me or my son what to do. Not in my backyard. That's just not going to happen.

As if Jake needs any of this shit. As if Jake is having the time of his goddamn life at that school. Jake's not exactly top of his class, let's say.

School isn't supposed to be fun. Wasn't for me. It's just something you have to go through, and you count down the days till it's over. And then when it is, hallefuckinglujah.

Jake's not ... Jake isn't exactly the brightest kid. And that's not his fault, okay? His old man's not exactly a bucket of brain power. And his mother, well ... His mother's something else.

That little asshole kid? Not the one with the gun, nope. The other one. Yeah. Yeah, that one. That kid. The dead kid. He stared at my boy Jake while he was changing. In the bloody locker room. Sure as hell did. And not like an accidental thing, not like he turned his head to look at the clock and got a peek of something he hadn't meant to. No. He said something about liking what he saw, just like that. "I like what I see." Like that's appropriate? Middle of the damn school day. And nobody said anything. Like that's allowed.

Just because you're different doesn't mean you're right.

And I didn't hear it from the coach. No he's tucked up nicely in his office dreaming about cheerleaders. He's not supervising. He's not making sure the kids aren't being assholes. Because, let's face it, kids are assholes a hell of a lot of the time. Whipping wet towels at each other. Whatever else. Smashing heads into lockers. This is something else. Whole fucking other ball of wax.

And what can I say to get one of those damn teachers' attention at school, huh? They just say it's a "sensitive issue." Yeah, that boy was all kinds of sensitive alright. They don't care one way or the other – to them it's just one of the school dumb-asses picking a fight with the fruit. And who's going to win there?

Fruit's word against Jake's. That's what it turns into.

If my son was a girl and some boy at school harassed him, imagine that! What the hell happens then, huh? It's all red flags then. Everyone's all flipped out then. Because we protect our daughters like there's no tomorrow because we're sure there's a rapist in an alley somewhere just drooling to get near her. But screw Jake, he's a big boy and he can take care of himself. And he could, sure, but it's not like the school's going to let him. Some little pansy is putting moves on my boy and oh, yeah, that's no problem. He's just "expressing himself." He's just figuring shit out. Well he's figuring out how to get the shit beat out of him.

Poor bastard's parents. Good luck with that. People talk about their kids being a handful. Yeah.

So what am I supposed to do now, right? Because it's sure as hell looking like I'm out of a job. And if I stop paying the rent then where does that leave Jake, huh? And I'll be damned if I can afford a lawyer. Even if I could he'd swindle me out of more money than I had, that's just the way it goes. You get charged a bazillion dollars for leaving a message on his voicemail and you think, for Christ's sake, I have a hard enough time with the price of a cup of coffee in the morning, never mind this bullshit. Did I ever choose the wrong kind of work. Could have made a million by now.

Jake's not scared. It's not like that. He's just checked out. He's just bottling up his anger. And I know anger. It can just take over. It's like shaking a soda can: eventually you're gonna open it, and then that shit's going to explode. It's going to get really messy before anything gets better. You can only tap on the bottom of the can so much, it's still not going to be happy when you open it.

Jake and I play videogames. It's our time together. You know, a couple hours a night. You got to limit that kind of thing, because God knows there are days I could play forever. Don't need to eat, don't need to shit, just let me game with my boy. And it's great, you know? Cuz you play a game where you finally get to drive over that bitch woman who won't cross the street fast enough when we're running late and it feels just great, doesn't it? I swear to God, there are days when I think that's the only thing that gets me through. Top scores for that too.

When the hell did we let the fags start running the world? I blame Obama for that one.

Kissing up to some ass-rider so that I can feed my boy. "Fuck you. You hear me? Fuck you! Fuck your company protocol. So I'm not allowed to speak my mind, is that it? Really, in my fucking United States, you're going to tell me I can't speak my mind. Good luck with that. I'll see you in court. I don't care. I don't need a damn lawyer, I'll represent myself. I have that right. If that's what it comes to. But tell you what, I'm coming in to work tomorrow, and you're not going to say shit about it, and I'll pick up my paycheque every Friday. I'm an American and I have the right to freedom of speech."

They're everywhere now, picking us off one by one because they've got an agenda and an easy ride. And me and Jake are the assholes? How in the hell do you figure that one? Wrap my head around that, I double dog dare you.

You put in fifteen years of good hard work. Fifteen years. Who the hell keeps the same job for fifteen years nowadays, what's what I wanna know. And then you say one word. You say one word that your faggot boss doesn't like and he wants you out on the doorstep. Bullshit. That kid is gone and dead now. Yes. He is. And on the one hand, that makes it easier for Jake.

But on the other hand. Fucking administration thinks it's all clean slate for that kid. See, because the school doesn't want to talk about the shit things that kid might have been doing in the locker room. Oh hell no. Now that he's dead he's going to become the school martyr. So great. Now all of this disappears off everyone's minds. Sure hasn't disappeared from Jake's, has it?

So I'm the asshole because I wanted to save my kid from that shit? Really? Really.

Maybe that kid with the gun needed to do what he did. Maybe that's the only way he could see the situation ending. Because when some asshole makes you feel worthless, makes you feel like a bag of shit nothing, where in the hell are you supposed to go from there, that's what I want to know. God only knows what had happened to him. It's the same damn locker room. Same damn coach.

I understand anger though.

No, you've got to teach a boy how to protect himself and his property. And take pride in himself. Even if you aren't the smartest. Well who in goddamn hell is? I sure wasn't, so what, I'm supposed to expect Jake to be shooting for the stars?

I'm not losing my job and my son. No way. Not happening.

So now I'm putting on a fucking tie and I'm going to go play lapdog to that asshole fruit who tried to fire me. Tried. Because I'm not going to roll over and just take it. I'm coming back, and I'm jumping through

whatever hoops he's asking me to. "I didn't mean what I said. It's just ...
It's complicated. My boy ..."

Because ...

Because things could have ended up really different. You know with Jake
and that kid. I'm just glad I keep my gun locked up.

HELEN:

> *HELEN is holding a glass of champagne at a celebration. It's late 2009, a year and a half later.*

Yes, cheers.

Cheers.

> *She drinks. And inevitably spills some champagne on herself.*

Sweet mother of ... Damnit!

> *She pulls out a tissue from her purse and starts mopping it up.*

See, this is why I don't drink red. Frank bought a Sparkling Shiraz for my birthday. Happy forty-third! He knows I like sparkling, but the Shiraz part I could have done without. It's still in the cupboard. Now we know why. Lord.

I'm sorry. Let's try it again, shall we?

> *She raises her glass.*

Better.

> *She continues mopping up the spill.*

Sometimes I just feel like Mary Poppins with everything I have in here. Chapstick?

> *She pulls out a tube of chapstick and applies some.*

Probably useless when I'm drinking. It's all going to smear on the lip of the glass, but oh well. At least then I'll be able to identify my glass when I inevitably lose it. "Which one? ... Oh, the one smeared with half a tube of Chapstick? ... Oh, right over there." At least I can feign that I'm rehydrating my lips. The more you talk, the more you need and there's so much to talk about that ...

This is a huge step. Huge. Momentous.

Everything always takes longer than it should. Than logic tells us it should take. That's just the nature of the world we live in, isn't it? But here we have it.

The Matthew Shepard and James Byrd Jr. Hate Crimes Prevention Act. There's weight even in its name.

How Judy Shepard spent eleven years trying to do right by her child's death but meeting nothing but bureaucratic opposition wherever she looked, I don't know. I've often wondered if her pushing for that long meant her being unable to move on. To turn the page and take control of her life. But then I suppose, how could you until the right thing has been done? And now here we are.

"Time heals all wounds," something like that.

And in the same year that our fine state decided to prevent homosexual couples from getting married. And we can joke and say, "Why would we want to deny them of that misery?" but ...

It's a step.

They didn't build the pyramids in a day. That old cliché still applies, doesn't it? We should probably stop using that one, though. No, they weren't built in a day, it took a lot longer than that, and quite a number of slaves. They like to downplay the slave part.

So what happens now?

Now we keep fighting for our students. That's what we do, we keep on fighting the good fight. And wait for the trial date.

I never imagined that we'd see this day before the trial has even started.

And I hate to be the downer. I know, it's a celebration, I know that. If I didn't I wouldn't have worn this champagne-soaked dress. Or is this sparkling? To be honest, I don't really know the difference. From France. Something like that. It's good, whatever it is.

As we're getting closer to the trial there's been a lot of talk in the papers regarding the killer being tried as an adult. A lot of people, people on both sides of the issue are crying foul. Even in the gay community. So maybe you can tell me what it's all about …

Let's see if I can stumble my way through this one. They're saying that children cannot be held accountable at the same psychological and neurological development levels as adults. That even teenagers, when in a state of intense emotion and fear, can lack the capacity to use reasoned judgment and prevent harmful action. Which to me just sounds like the gay-panic argument all over again.

And given that the killer was only nineteen days into being fourteen at the time …

I mean I read all of that and part of me thinks yes, absolutely, I've had my fair share of students and can definitely say that their development is key, that they don't have all the answers immediately and that that process continues on into their teens. But it continues on past that. Past fifteen, past eighteen, past thirty even. So where do we draw the line? A number doesn't necessarily dictate an intention. I didn't intend to spill all over myself, did I? But I still did it. It still happened.

And in the arraignment the judge even referred to him as shooting "with the cold-blooded precision of an executioner." So you tell me, does that sound like a child's confusion?

I'm getting heavy-handed. And I don't mean to, but …

I just still have a need to talk. Frank doesn't want to, and I get that, there's a lot on his plate as well. There's a lot on everyone's plate. And my car broke down today, just to make everything better. Smooth ride, right? So it's never the right time to talk about things, so you end up at parties having a conversation that isn't exactly what people are hoping for. But isn't this what we're celebrating, ultimately? Something that will make all the difference in the trial?

The Matthew Shepard and James Byrd Jr. Hate Crimes Prevention Act. I just like saying it. Saying it reminds me that it's real.

If the trial is successful – which I truly hope it is, and with so many witnesses, it surely will be – our young murderer will not see the outside of a cell until his sixty-fifth birthday. And the part of me that misses my dead student, the part of me that registers that loss stands firm in believing in that. If you are old enough to conceive of getting even, to take a relative's gun and wait for your victim, then shoot him twice, you are no child.

I keep telling Frank that yes, yes, I'm emotional when I talk about this. He keeps repeating that. "Helen," he says, "Helen, this isn't your cause. I understand that you're upset and emotional, but you're so much on the periphery. You need to pour your energy into something else, hon." He's a lovely, gentle man – and he's worried that I'll get so swept up in my own rage that him and our relationship will just disappear. But I think this is the clearest Helen voice I've ever had.

I truly have a hard time believing that he was confused by his own actions. It's too easy to say that he was simply too young to know what he was doing.

And maybe I would change my mind if it were my child. If I were staring at the possibility that I wouldn't touch my child's face for a lifetime. I don't know what that moment would feel like. That realization. But I'm not a parent.

Frank never wanted kids. I don't think I could have carried them anyway, from what I hear. There's not enough tea tree in the world for that one. But in a way I suppose not having kids is what brought me into teaching. It's like parenting: half the time you're banging your head against a wall to get your point across, but then you get these intimate moments when you can make a difference. When just listening goes so far.

And I can imagine that if that moment, the moment you realize you're going to lose your child, feels anything like that moment the day after the shooting, reading about all of this in the paper, realizing that you'll never see one of your favourite students again, well then I don't envy her, the mother.

But that pain is not something that I can save her from, or we can save her from. That is a pain she needs to feel.

We're just a series of choices. That's all we are, as people. Our parents are only responsible for so much of who we become. We're just flesh and spirit and choice.

My parents never hit me. Never once, except one day when for whatever reason, I was about three years old at the time, I decided to run out of the house, directly into traffic. But I ran, full tilt, directly onto a busy street. And I could have died. Right then and there, easily. I logically should have. But the drivers were attentive and swerved and slammed on their brakes. And my mother ran out chasing me, and she grabbed me and she hit me, a few times, in fact. And she should have. Because I had done something extremely dangerous, and irrational, and wrong. And that's how we learn.

That boy will not get the death penalty. But he will get those hits in his own way.

Let's have another glass, no? I'm weighing you down with all of this. We need to celebrate first, smile first, and then get heavy later. I'm doing it all backwards, aren't I?

ROGER:

*ROGER, thirty-three, sits at his desk. It's
lunch hour and he drinks a cup of coffee.*

You're not about to convince me of the fact that he deserved to be
heralded as a hero. Oh Christ no. That kid was, at best, someone who
really could have used a special-education program at our school.
Something more intensive, more one-on-one for kids with difficulties.
We can't say disabilities nowadays, it's not PC, but ultimately for the fuck-
ups who we're trying to prevent from being just who they are.

Because let's call it like it is. He was a shit disturber. And our school
doesn't need more of those. Everyone's starved for attention all the
time. It's the crux of being a teenager, isn't it? Being self-involved and
self-important. And fine, yes, when you don't fit in, then all of a sudden
you have this need to either hide it or scream your difference from the
rooftops. And Christ did he do a bang-up job of that.

*ROGER takes a chocolate bar out
of his desk and unwraps it.*

It's not exactly a balanced diet, but it gets you through the day. Sugar and
caffeine.

*He has a sip of coffee and bites into the chocolate,
which he continues eating throughout.*

Ah. Nice. Better. There are days when I spend the entire morning craving
this forty minutes of bliss. Undisturbed. For the most part. I avoid the
staff room entirely. I don't want to catch up with the other teachers about
their families, their problem students, what we're going to do for the staff
Christmas party, none of that. I want to leave that at the sound of the bell.
This is my time. Me time.

See, here's the thing. How in the hell are we expected to teach thirty
kids when one of them makes that impossible? That's what I want to
know. And no, it's not just a "challenge" for teachers like me, it's not

this awakening, enlightening moment that really makes us discover why we came into the teaching profession. Dig down deep into our core of patience and push through his inability to focus and his determination to make everyone in the room stare at him at all times. No. School isn't a fucking fashion show. It's not a pageant and it's not a free-for-all.

Think of it this way, right: If every girl I had in that class decided to come to school dressed like a little tart and paraded around trying to get a reaction out of the bad boys, there would be intervention, am I wrong? Please, tell me I'm wrong. That would get a reaction out of the higher-ups. That would be the talk of the staff room. We'd pause our Secret Santa plans to discuss that one. But no. Not quite. Does one student's egomaniacal behaviour automatically trump all of the others? Is it within his right to prevent them from getting a decent education, all in the name of supposed "self-expression"? That's a tough sell for me.

We work long hours. Longer than we should, really. When you look at the extracurriculars, and sure, fine, we don't "have" to do them, but then you're the asshole teacher who isn't devoted enough, and the minute you need something from the principal you're not going to get it because you're not showing dedication. So you just skip that battle altogether and say "Fine," and you end up supervising something or coaching something. Something low-key – library club maybe, debate team. No, not debate team. That was one year that would just never end. Never again. Lesson learned on that one.

And all of that just makes this forty minutes worth it. It's like a finish line. You've earned them. And you're going to use up every last second of those minutes.

It's not the gay thing. People automatically hear what I'm saying and they want to dismiss it, they want it to be "Oh, some asshole bigot who snuck under the radar of teachers' college," but no, at fifteen I think most of these kids will hump whatever is willing, and go to it, kids. Wear a condom, but go to it. That kid being gay, so publicly wanting the world to acknowledge that he was gay, isn't what made him a problem. There are other gay kids at this school, they just have a sense of what's appropriate where. Some decorum. Because let's be honest here, not everyone can do whatever they want whenever they want, that's just not a possibility.

I'm sorry. That's the world we live in. And I'm not saying it's fair, but I'm saying it's true.

And what's appropriate here isn't some boy wearing makeup and heels, it's really not. Because nobody is focusing on arithmetic when that walks into the room. Nobody should actually be expected to just push through and persevere when that's trying to overwhelm them and take up any bit of focus they had coming into class.

I'm sorry, but if we're being honest he was a hazard to every kid in that classroom. He was a wild card. You truly never knew what he was going to do next. And though some of my colleagues found it brave, or fascinating, he was not our school pop star. He was not someone they should all have been gossiping about in the staff room. That's not what it's for. He made enough of a mark in the class. The staff room is to get out of that mode. To feel like a human being for a few minutes midday so that you can continue on with half a smile through the afternoon. And when the whole staff room has become just this gossip pool, really not all that different from the hallways filled with students nattering about what he's done this time, then there's a problem.

He was just another kid with a bad home life who wanted to take it out on the rest of us.

School is quieter now, frankly. Kids are quieter. It changes things. Can't ignore that. It takes time for people to calm down. Computer lab's still closed. I think out of respect more than anything.

More school counsellors around too. Kids need to talk it out. Good, I'm glad they've brought someone in for that. Important.

And the principal's asking, "Why aren't you taking some time off, Rog. We could swing a couple weeks. See your wife, give your daughters a squeeze." But I'm good.

Sugar and caffeine for forty minutes is the only time off I need. You can't let everything shake you up. Life goes on. It just finds a way.

He takes a final bite of the chocolate.

It's amazing how much that'll fill you up. Not for the whole day, but it gets you through that hump hour. Makes sure you don't hit that wall. There are too many personalities in the room for you to afford to hit the wall. Some of them are just waiting for a moment when you have your guard down.

So you make sure you're on guard when he's in class. That's for sure.

Look, we definitely have kids at our school who are drifters, who've never quite found their place in the social strata. Every school's got them. I like to think of them like driftwood, that over time, these kids will smooth out their rough edges. And then, of course, we have those determined academic kids, the books, who aren't interested in the social games that high school inevitably plays. Good for them, I think. The books. Good for them. It takes a lot of effort not to get involved.

There are other difficult kids. Not hard in that they demand all of the attention, but in that they're a bit lost. They're the ones who struggle academically despite having glowing social abilities – they're magazines, these kids. Glossy, but vacant. And when you have an empty building and you fill it with driftwood, books, and magazines, you can only imagine what can happen.

And that kid was a spark.

RHONDA:

*RHONDA, a mile-a-minute eleven-year-old, lies
in a hospital bed, rubbing her exposed stomach.*

Tuna sandwiches give you the worst breath imaginable. Worse than
coffee. Worse than beer. People should know that. People should know
that the eating of tuna sandwiches is not a social act. They should not
chew them in people's faces. Shouldn't lean in to kiss them hello or
goodbye mid-bite. I can't stand tuna sandwiches. They invite getting
familiar with someone's insides. Hospital vending machines are full of
them. Either because they don't go bad or because nobody likes them.
Maybe both. But there I am, staring into that glass cubicled machine – it's
like a prison for unwanted snacks: bruised apples, pudding cups with tiny
spoons, and tuna sandwiches. And yeah, sure, I'm hungry. But if these are
my only options ...

I know, hospitals feed you. I know that. I've been in and out of the
hospital for as long as I can remember, but you get sick of cream-
of-everything soup. And a meal that's made two states over, frozen,
and shipped. I was hoping for something else. Something better. But
somehow I'm confronted with tuna.

Adoption records aren't perfect, I'll tell you that much. Filling out a form
about medical history – how am I supposed to know? How are my dads?
My mom was from somewhere in Canada. Canada's awfully big. I know
her name was Leslie, but what? I can't exactly canvas door to door in
Canada asking for Leslie's liver history, can I?

Hospitals smell like hopelessness. And question marks. Don't you think?
I lie here just waiting, just counting down, and all I want is to go to the
movies. My dads had promised to take me to the movies before we came
in, to see anything I wanted within ratings limits. BORING! All the good
stuff is at least PG-13. But it didn't work out. All I know is if Dad One
didn't plan so much, Dad Two wouldn't find a way to mess those plans up
so often. "Maybe that's why I'm only second in command, kiddo," he says,
which is our joke. Some people think it's odd that I number my dads,
but "Papa" sounds like a grandpa, "Pappy" sounds like a pervert's name,

"Pops" sounds like a barber, "Daddy" is for kids, and so numerically I find a way out of it.

So no movies for me. But they said they'll rent me one of those hospital-bed TVs. Not quite the same, is it?

It's the night before. And I watch the seconds tick by. Nervously. I'm practically a basket case. That word has never made sense to me, but I still use it because it seems that it's the socially accepted word for what I'm feeling. It's not that I'm scared. No doctor's ever been able to defeat me. I'm practically invincible. But it's more a looming sense that something about all of this isn't good. That something horrible is happening and that there's nothing I can do about it because here I am, stuck in a hospital bed, eyeballing the second hand.

And I worry. I worry about scarring. Because girls with scars can't become supermodels. Because I pretty much have everything else I need to do it. You can't strut down a runway if you've got weird bits on your body. Nobody likes that. Not in the fashion industry. And I would know. Because Dad Two bought me a designer dress last time I was in hospital because he was out of town and couldn't make it back for a couple days. But they're both here now. Just sitting by me.

People think it's weird. Having two dads. They worry I don't have a maternal influence. They don't say that. Not exactly. But every so often a mother smiles at my dads, but gives me this look that suggests she wants to nurse me. I can't decide whether it's incredibly creepy or incredibly sad. Likely both. It doesn't bug me though. If that's what a maternal influence means, I think I'll risk not having one.

Nobody has two parents nowadays anyway. Lots of people have one, or four, or some elaborate mathematical equation that explains how many they have and how they're all related. "Step" this and "half" that. That's more complicated than anything I'm dealing with. It's just two dads and a sort-of mom somewhere off in the distance. A Canadian mom.

Time ticks away and I wake up with the sweats. I've never had them, but it keeps me stirring. And Dad One mops my forehead and Dad Two brings in the nurse. "I don't have a fever, just a fervent dream cycle." They smile. They smile at my use of language and my ability to make them smile. I'm freaking out but smiling for their sake. I'd imagine the only thing harder than going under the knife is watching your kid do it. Waiting. Just waiting.

And as I wait I start seeing you. And I want you to sing me a song. Just to fill the air in here. Hospitals are the loudest and quietest places. So sing me something familiar and if I feel up to it, I'll sing along. Something beautiful and about love. But not about the loss of it. I've had enough of the loss of things. That would be what they call kicking a dead horse, which is awful, when you think about it. Why would you kick a horse anyway? Though I suppose it would have to be dead if you were gonna actually kick it. Horses tend to be better at kicking than getting kicked.

Still, sing even if you're off-key. It won't matter as long as you're passionate. And you need a certain amount of passion to sing at all, right? My dads sing in the quaintest little harmony. It's not supposed to be harmony. I'm pretty sure they think it's unison, but Dad One just has no idea what he's doing. Which makes it better, in a way. Because it keeps it real and heartfelt. Dad Two just keeps adjusting the melody to try to make it fit. Dad Two hates it when he sings along, but I think it's just about perfect.

Sing me a song now and hopefully I'll fall asleep and dream about all of it being over.

But then it's time. The big day, the nurse calls it. I force a smile.

His breath is recognizable beneath his paper mask. And I drift off into another world with only one thing on my mind: tuna sandwiches. Tooth brushing should be mandatory for surgeons.

RHONDA rises from the bed.

Count backwards from ten but I hit seven and I'm gone. I see you. You hold my hand while I'm drifting away, keep holding it as I'm walking down the runway in Dad Two's fancy dress.

> *She folds her sheet into a fancy dress on her body and struts down an imagined catwalk. Music plays. Cameras flash.*

People snap photos. They can't help themselves because we're too beautiful together, hand in hand. I pose. And you pose. And it looks like you've been practising. You move flawlessly in your own dress, and you've mastered that broken-doll pose. And just as I'm getting the hang of it, you squeeze my hand to bring me back to Earth. And already I miss that dream. My no-scar supermodel dream.

She lies back down in bed.

But my eyes open. My dads are there, arms all intertwined, fast asleep.

They put one of your organs inside me. Isn't that strange? Isn't it just the weirdest thing? They can do that.

Type A's a weird blood group. Which is odd because A is one of the most common letters in the alphabet. You'd think they'd give a weird blood type Q or K. But it's A.

It keeps me company, though. It's just a liver. I know that. But if I really focus, which I do, I can almost hear a voice. The voice of this lost boy. A voice in the dark, echoing in my thoughts and telling me: "Rhonda … Rhonda, it will be okay. It will."

Maybe that voice is my dads'. Maybe it's both of them. But I like to think it's you.

HELEN:

*Present day. HELEN sits in her
apartment, coffee in hand.*

Damn. Damn. Damn.

So I don't know. That's the bottom line.

I never really know.

Is that my fatal flaw? My inability to decide. Am I a fence sitter?

It just gets uglier with time, don't you think? When it all first happens
you're craving more information, all of the whys and hows, but then when
they come out in the open, when the dirty laundry is thrown out into the
world you just want to shrink away. Details are horrible things. When it's
vague you have questions, but that's better than being confronted with
the reality.

What reality? I can't say these past years have been a reality. There's just
no way. There's just no way to actually look at ...

And work. Ha. What work? I get so caught up in ...

He haunts me.

Frank used to call me the "eternal optimist." Not anymore, though.
Not anymore.

No.

There's only so much attention a person has to give out, right? There's
only so much output of energy that we're capable of as human beings.
That's the truth of it. It's basic math, anyone who's ever been on a diet
knows that – intake of calories versus output. Well, the same goes for
spirit, I think. The same goes for emotion.

So something happens that you realize you need to pour yourself into and you do. And then other things end up falling by the wayside because they don't have quite the same value for other people that they do for you. And then the wayside just gets further and further away until it's nothing. Gone.

And I did. And he is.

You organize and organize and for what? I mean it, for what? Meetings and petitions and rallies, they don't do anything, do they? They're just tools that we're told are within our rights to make us feel like we're still alive and have a say in things. But we don't. And I think we secretly know that. But confronting that tiny piece of truth is horrifying.

We are not within control of our own lives.

When I first heard the news ... When was that? I was angry. More than angry. Deflated and shaking and sucker-punched. How could anyone not be? You don't want to see that on the news. You don't want to hear that at all, but you at least want someone to phone you and tell you that your life has changed.

And yet it's no different even now. Lives are ruined. They only become more so. And it was a harmless game, really. Girls play it in the schoolyard all of the time. Kiss and tell. Worse, nowadays. Coloured bracelets that represent all kinds of lewd so-called accomplishments. This was rather innocent by comparison. Even for him. Just a valentine. Just "Be my valentine." Nothing big. What's a valentine to a boy? A funny little valentine becomes a domino to something bigger than all of us. And then a child is no more. At least in body, but he has come to exist in so much more – in thoughts and voices in late nights of disrupted sleep, sweat-stained sheets because the body feels the stresses of an atmosphere riddled with vibrations, these tiny ripples that tell us that something's not good, the universe is sending the message, our brains, our tears, our hearts feel it and the message is clear: Something has to change.

This is what life feels like.

And the delays and endless delays. And then finally the trial ... The waiting and watching and bated breath. I sat and I listened. Listened to things that nobody would ever want to hear because with each word you end up feeling more and more sick. More incapable of tempering yourself. Of biting your tongue and cooling your jets and staying in your seat. Mute has never been one of my states of being. But I listened. I didn't want to hear it, but I also didn't want a root canal last spring, did I? I also don't want to be on a diet. Life is full of things we don't want. That's what it feels like.

Wow.

And the second trial. And the verdict. Twenty-one years. Is that what a life's worth? I don't know. I really don't. Who does, but. But nothing, really. Nothing specific. Just "but." "But" everything. Just a general complaint, a calling foul, an acknowledgment that no right has come out of this, that the end of a trial is not the end of anything really. The only closure is for the press because they're off to the next gay teen suicide. The next Columbine, the next Sandy Hook. These stories that keep appearing time and time again as if nothing has happened. As if nothing is any different now than nine years ago, when ... "But." I can't sift through it all to figure out what my objection is, but there is an objection tucked up in there. There is.

And the books and documentary, and analysis pieces. The crime fiction. It's not forgotten. Maybe pushed aside, but it's still there.

It's not juvenile detention anymore for that kid. That was ages ago. After he turned eighteen, it was the big leagues. Prison time. That's nice. That he could turn eighteen. That he still had that ability.

Yes, I'm drinking coffee again. I was off it for a while. Caffeine. It's not supposed to be good. You know what else isn't? Divorce at forty-five. No, I know that life goes on. Sure. Yes. It's supposed to, isn't it? There are the phases of grief, aren't there? Lovely. You know, to cope with ...

I'm not his ... I know. I know that.

But I still see him you know. It's not a vision. That's not what I mean. I'm not a religious person. Got that out of my system in my youth. Some try LSD, I tried G-O-D. It had the same effect. You get high and disillusioned.

But despite not believing in, well, whatever religion wants us all to believe, I do feel him. In my sleep, in the air. I breathe him into my lungs and see him everywhere I go. In the eyes of every student I see who's different, who doesn't just lie down and take whatever shit the universe wants to dish out at them. Whatever subtle signals of "you don't belong" they're being given. He lives in them.

Not my students. I'm taking some time off. But they never quite leave you, do they? He's so far out of reach and never quite gone.

I should warm this cup up, or something. Lukewarm coffee is pretty much rock bottom.

> *She spills it on herself again.*

Oh for Christ's sake.

> *She stands.*

> **THE COLLECTOR** *examines his surroundings and exits.*

> *Blackout.*

LADIES AND GENTLEMEN,
BOYS AND GIRLS

PRODUCTION HISTORY

Ladies and Gentlemen, Boys and Girls was first produced by Roseneath Theatre and toured throughout the province of Ontario, Canada, from March 19 to May 4, 2018, with the following cast and crew:

FIN	Samson Brown
MOM, HOLLY, and **TEACHER**	athena kaitlin trinh
DAD and **FELIX**	Matthew Finlan

Director	Andrew Lamb
Set and Costume Designer	Anna Treusch
Design Assistant	Sim Suzer
Sound Designer	Verne Good
Artistic Director	Andrew Lamb
Stage Manager	Alice Ferreyra
Management Director	Annemieke Wade
Production Manager	Courtney Pyke
Associate Producer	Nicole Myers Mitchell
Education and Marketing Manager	Gretel Meyer Odell

PRODUCTION NOTE

Ladies and Gentlemen, Boys and Girls takes place in multiple locations, with scenes unfolding into one another. Think multiple circus acts happening in three rings in tandem. Very rarely is there any need for a physical indication of location. The action moves quickly and briskly, sometimes jumping in time or in location with the flick of a wrist.

The play's scenes all bleed into each other with **FIN** addressing the audience directly throughout.

CHARACTERS

ACTOR 1, trans boy / genderqueer

> **FIN**: nine years old, assigned female at birth and named Fiona, but coming out trans as Fin, a trans boy; Fin also appears in memory at age five

ACTOR 2, female

> **MOM** (Sharon): Fin's mom, having a hard time with Fin's recent coming out

> **HOLLY**: twelve years old, Fin's sister; she also appears in memory at age eight

> **TEACHER**: Fin's new grade-four teacher

ACTOR 3, male

> **DAD** (Stuart): Fin's dad and main support system

> **FELIX**: nine years old, Fin's new school friend

athena kaitlin trinh as Mom, Samson Brown as Fin, and Matthew Finlan as Dad in Roseneath Theatre's 2018 premiere production tour of *Ladies and Gentlemen, Boys and Girls*.

Matthew Finlan as Felix, Samson Brown as Fin, and athena kaitlin trinh as Holly in Roseneath Theatre's 2018 premiere production.

Photos by John Packman, courtesy of Roseneath Theatre.

Scene One: Pre-Show Entertainment

> *FIN enters and speaks directly to audience,*
> *inviting them into the play.*

FIN: Looking back, I'd say it all started when I decided to cut my hair.

> *MOM and DAD enter. An over-the-top, almost clown-like*
> *duo. They're grounded in real heart, but are larger than life.*

MOM: Honey!

DAD: Buddy!

MOM: Sweetheart?

DAD: Fiona!

MOM: Fiona! We're going to be late, come on honey.

DAD: Fiona! I'm already in the car!

MOM: Fiona! Your breakfast is an iceberg by now.

DAD: Fiona! The keys are in the ignition.

MOM: Fiona! I've already got one shoe on.

DAD: Fiona! The car's creeping down the driveway.

FIN: I hear you! I know!

> *FIN arrives in front of his parents, and*
> *reveals his new short haircut.*

DAD: What in the world?

MOM: Fiona, where on Earth is your hair?

DAD: You didn't!

MOM: Because I certainly don't see it anywhere on your head!

DAD: You did?!

MOM: That better be some kind of a wig, young lady.

DAD: Do you really think it could be a wig?

MOM: Well I don't know. I'm just trying to make some sense of it.

DAD: Come on, that can't be a wig.

MOM: So you really chopped it all off?

FIN: I think it looks better like this.

MOM: Better? It was so pretty before.

FIN: I don't want to look pretty.

MOM: Well then you've definitely achieved that.

DAD: Sharon!

MOM: What?

DAD inspects the haircut.

DAD: Wait a minute, did you do this all by yourself?

FIN: Yeah.

DAD: That's pretty impressive.

MOM: Stuart!

DAD: Well it is. It's remarkably even. Look at the back! I have trouble shaving my face, never mind cutting the hair on the back of my head!

MOM: But honestly, Stuart, you're telling me that you actually approve of what she's done?

DAD: It's definitely bold.

MOM: Bold! Definitely.

DAD: It's a statement.

MOM: I'll say.

DAD: Quite the statement!

MOM: A loud statement! Fiona, I really wish you'd mentioned this before ...

DAD: Well I think it looks great.

FIN: Thanks.

MOM: Stuart!

DAD: What?

MOM: Do you?

DAD: I do!

MOM: I certainly hope you didn't use my good sewing scissors to cut it.

FIN: Well –

MOM: Fiona!

DAD: It's fine.

MOM: Stuart!

DAD: What?

MOM: Those are my good scissors!

DAD: And thanks to them, Fiona has a great new look.

MOM: Fiona, get in the car. We're late!

DAD: But not so late that we aren't hitting the Tim's drive-thru.

MOM: Stuart!

DAD: What? It's time for hot chocolate!

MOM: But we're late!

DAD: And we're celebrating.

MOM: Celebrating what?

DAD: The impressive new hair stylist in the family.

FIN: (*interrupting the scene and speaking to the audience*) No, it was before that. It must have been. Not that I can really place it. It's just always been there. There wasn't one big moment, it was always there. I knew it. I could feel it.

Scene Two: Three Ring Circus

FIN ushers us into a memory.

FIN: I remember when I was five and my dad announced that he had –

DAD: The biggest surprise for my girls. Go get ready, we're going out!

FIN: We had no idea where we were going, but Saturday morning cartoons were over, so we were ready for anything.

HOLLY: Can we get snacks?

FIN: Holly, my sister. Always with the snacks.

DAD: Maybe.

HOLLY: Can I wear my princess dress?

DAD: If you really, really want to.

FIN: We loaded into the car, Dad in the front, me and Holly in the back.

HOLLY: Shotgun!

FIN: (*to HOLLY*) It's not "shotgun" when we're both sitting in the back.

HOLLY: Backgun!

FIN: (*to the audience*) We drove across town and arrived in front of the biggest tent I'd ever seen in my life. And the lineup! I'd never seen so many people in line. Like a Boxing Day sale! Families all waiting to get into this massive tent. The size of a school gym.

HOLLY: The size of a parking lot.

FIN: (*to HOLLY*) The size of the mall.

HOLLY: The size of infinity.

FIN: Sure, Holly. (*to the audience*) That's when Holly spotted the sign.

HOLLY: The Doberman Brothers' Majestic Circus.

FIN and HOLLY: CIRCUS!!!

> *Classic Barnum & Bailey, big-top circus music plays.*

FIN: I'd never been so excited. Not for cartoons –

HOLLY: Or back-to-school shopping!

FIN: Or waffles!

HOLLY: Or drive-thru hot chocolate!

FIN: The tent had more seats than I'd ever seen. It was like a whole school assembly in a tent!

HOLLY: A church in a tent.

FIN: A stadium in a tent.

HOLLY: A city in a tent.

FIN: Not quite. (*to the audience*) Seats all around the centre-stage area with three rings.

HOLLY: What's with the rings?

DAD: It's a three-ring circus!

HOLLY: Like three-ring binders?

DAD: Sort of.

HOLLY: I want onion rings!

FIN: (*to HOLLY and DAD*) But the show's gonna start!

HOLLY: I want popcorn!

FIN: (*to HOLLY*) Aren't you afraid the lions might attack you for it?!

HOLLY: There's lions?!

DAD: Maybe!

HOLLY: Will they really attack?!

FIN: One hundred percent absolutely they will!

DAD: Don't scare your sister.

HOLLY: Do lions even like popcorn?

FIN: I dunno, but do you really want to risk it?

DAD: Good call. We wouldn't want to lose one of you to the circus, right? It's like we always say ...

FIN: "If the whole family isn't in the boat –"

HOLLY: "– then it starts to sink instead of float."

DAD: Exactly! So maybe we should wait for the intermission, just in case.

FIN: What's the intermission? Is that like some kind of special mission?

HOLLY: An underwater-mermaid mission?!

FIN: A space-voyage-to-Mars mission?!

HOLLY: A supermodel-runway-fashion-show mission?

FIN: Sure, Holly.

DAD: The intermission is the break in the middle of the show. We'll get our popcorn then.

HOLLY: Would a boat really not float without everyone in it?

DAD: Well, it's a make-believe boat.

FIN: (*to the audience*) We shuffled into our seats just as the lights dimmed and for the first time in her life, Holly was completely quiet.

> FIN *and* DAD *stare at* HOLLY.
> *Nothing. She's transfixed.*

FIN: The music played, then all of a sudden a spotlight hit the centre ring, and standing there was a tiny person in a glittery top hat and long-tailed coat. Bright red. As soon as they opened their mouth, I thought, "That's a girl!"

HOLLY: No it's not!

FIN: (*to HOLLY*) I think it is.

HOLLY: It's not.

FIN: Why?

HOLLY: Because of the suit and hat.

FIN: Girls can't wear suits and hats?

HOLLY: Not like that.

FIN: That doesn't even make sense.

HOLLY: You don't even make sense.

FIN: (*to the audience*) Arguing has never been Holly's strong suit. She's three years older, but if you ask me, she isn't three years smarter.

The show started! (*as the circus's ring leader*) Ladies and gentlemen, boys and girls, the Doberman Brothers proudly present their Majestic Three Ring Circus! Feast your eyes on the wonderment!

We hear more whimsical circus soundscape.

DAD: Having fun?

HOLLY and **FIN:** SHHHH!

DAD: Sorry, sorry!

FIN: The show was magnificent. Magical. Marvellous!

HOLLY: Meh.

FIN: She's just pretending not to care. She loved the trapeze artists as they swung from their little perches up near the highest point of the big top.

HOLLY: Don't fall!!!

FIN: Dad loved watching the lion tamer as he stuck his head inside this majestic beast's mouth without getting it chomped off.

DAD: I can't watch! I can't watch!

HOLLY: I'm glad we didn't get popcorn!

FIN: See! (*to the audience*) But all I could think about was that girl in the top hat. The ring leader. The one in charge. I'd only ever seen pictures of a circus and the person in the top hat was always a man. Every time.

HOLLY: I still think that's a boy.

FIN: Just because you think so doesn't make it true.

HOLLY: You're not true.

FIN: Sure, Holly. (*to the audience*) The circus had everything. Ring leader, trapeze, lion tamer ... that was only the beginning! Jugglers!

DAD: Are those bowling pins?!

HOLLY: Woah, are those swords?!

DAD: Now they're on fire!

FIN: Then clowns, which still totally creep me out.

DAD: How many of them can they fit in that car?

FIN: But then they introduced one of their top acts. A larger-than-life figure who entered, backlit, to tumultuous applause. (*as ring leader*) Ladies and Gentlemen, Boys and Girls, the Doberman Brothers' Majestic Circus proudly presents our very own wonder of the world, the one, the only Bearded Lady of Leftuvia!

Explosion of applause.

HOLLY: How is that a lady?

FIN: (*to HOLLY*) What do you mean?

HOLLY: Well, she has a beard.

FIN: So?

HOLLY: I don't know. Isn't that weird? Dad used to have a beard.

FIN: So?

HOLLY: Dad's a man.

FIN: Yeah, so?

HOLLY: Maybe it's because she's from Leftuvia?

FIN: (*to the audience*) I'd never even heard of Leftuvia. But I knew I'd never seen anything like it. She was beautiful and elegant.

HOLLY: Look at her dress!

FIN: I didn't fully understand what I was looking at. Who knew confusion could be so exciting?

HOLLY: Dad, is that really a lady?

DAD: Well, she's called the Bearded Lady, isn't she? So I guess she's a lady.

HOLLY: She doesn't look like a lady.

DAD: Maybe it's not about how she looks.

FIN: I don't think he really knew then how important that statement was. Of course, Holly wasn't impressed.

HOLLY: Do you think she'll let me try on her dress?

DAD: I guess we'll have to wait and see.

FIN: The Bearded Lady. My head was spinning. I don't know why. But something about her was like a fire lighting up in me. At the break –

DAD: The intermission!

FIN: – I couldn't contain my excitement. It was like I'd eaten an entire bag of Halloween candy mixed with a whole pot of coffee and finished off with a Red Bull. I had so many questions! WOOOO HOOOO!

HOLLY: Calm down. Jeez!

FIN: (*to HOLLY*) Do you think I could grow a beard?

HOLLY: Ew! No!

FIN: (*to the audience*) Dad finally bought us popcorn and cotton candy.

HOLLY: My fingers are sticky!

DAD: Just lick them clean.

HOLLY: Ew! No!

FIN: (*to HOLLY*) I'll do it.

> *FIN goes to lick HOLLY's fingers. She's repulsed.*

HOLLY: No you won't! Gross! Stop being such a boy!

FIN: (*to the audience*) It was meant as an insult. But it sure didn't feel like one.

DAD: Want to bring that popcorn back into the show?

HOLLY: Uh-uh, too risky.

FIN: (*to HOLLY*) Yeah, maybe there's bears in the second half! (*to the audience*) We finished our popcorn and Holly gave up on the rest of the cotton candy.

HOLLY: It's too sweet.

FIN: (*to HOLLY*) Isn't that kind of the point? (*to the audience*) I've never really understood her.

> *FIN puts the rest of the cotton candy on his face as if it's a beard.*

FIN: (*to HOLLY and DAD*) Hey look, I'm the Bearded Lady of Leftuvia.

DAD: You sure are! All you need is the dress.

HOLLY: I want the dress!

FIN: (*to the audience*) And we climbed back into our seats.

HOLLY: Are the trapezes gonna do more tricks?

DAD: Not sure, love.

HOLLY: I'm getting bored.

FIN: (*to HOLLY*) Of course you are. (*to the audience*) But even Holly's boredom couldn't take away from this incredible feeling creeping over me. The second act was amazing. Dog tricks! More clowns, and then the Ringleader wheeled out this huge pool of water, like a giant goldfish tank. I kept thinking maybe they had a shark. I couldn't wait to see the look on Holly's face if she had to watch a real live shark. Maybe they'd even feed it some fish and there'd be blood in the water and Holly would have a horror show meltdown.

HOLLY: AHHHHH!!

FIN: But instead, all of a sudden there were these two creatures swimming in formation, dancing in the water. So beautiful. So scaly!

HOLLY: Mermaids!

FIN: With the longest hair I'd ever seen. Holly and I both sat mesmerized.

HOLLY: Look at their hair!

FIN: (*to HOLLY and DAD*) Look at their fins!

HOLLY: Look at their tails!

DAD: Pretty great stuff, huh girls?

FIN: When I grow up I want to be a mermaid.

HOLLY: Me too!

DAD: Two mermaids in the family, huh? I guess your mother and I better buy a boat!

HOLLY: Yeah, and all of us need to be in it or it'll sink, right?

FIN: (*to the audience*) I couldn't stop staring. I'd never much thought about mermaids before. I'd seen the Disney movie, but here, in person, everything started to change. But why? What was it?

At the end of the show I was up on my feet cheering: "YAY! AMAZING! BRAVO!" We came home from the circus and I spent weeks pretending to be that Ringleader. Standing on the coffee table, welcoming an invisible audience of families to my living room. "Step right up, step right up. Find your seats and welcome to the Greatest Show you'll ever feast your eyes on. Boy are you in for a treat! You want clowns? We got 'em. Bearded ladies in beaded gowns? Trapeze artists? No problem. Contortionists and strong men, lions, and bears. There's even some creatures you've never heard of. Unique, original, and all under the big top."

And weeks became months and months became years and soon, Ringleader's Circus was my favourite game.

Scene Three: Mermaids

We return to the present with **FIN** *standing on the living room's coffee table, with a mock ringleader costume on.* **HOLLY** *enters, smartphone in hand. She's all bossy tween.*

HOLLY: Oh my God, are you still doing that?

FIN: Um –

HOLLY: Who are you even talking to?

FIN: My legions of fans!

HOLLY: You're ridiculous.

FIN: So what?

HOLLY: It's weird.

FIN: It's not any weirder than playing *Candy Crush Saga* all the time.

HOLLY: It's way weirder.

FIN: Really? Making stuff up is weirder than getting so excited about new emojis?

HOLLY: At least when I'm texting, it's with real people.

FIN: The circus is coming back to town and Dad said we could go.

HOLLY: Who cares?

FIN: Me.

HOLLY: Well I don't.

FIN: Look, Holly, if you're gonna sit here, then play the trapeze artist.

HOLLY: Be your own trapeze artist.

FIN: I'm the Ringleader.

HOLLY: You don't even have the hat.

FIN: Come on!

HOLLY: Not gonna happen.

FIN: (*as ring leader*) Ladies and Gentlemen, Boys and Girls, feast your eyes on my sister Holly! Watch her as she contorts her tongue into hideous faces and moves her thumbs across the screen at record speed! Watch her pretend she doesn't care that the circus is coming back to town.

HOLLY: I'm not pretending. Move, I want to watch TV.

FIN: Just watch something on your phone.

HOLLY: The screen's too small. Move!

FIN: No!

HOLLY: You're so annoying.

FIN: Is there an emoji for that?

HOLLY: Ugh, whatever. You want me to play? Fine, I'll swim around and be the mermaid.

FIN: It's not time for the mermaid now. I haven't even brought out the tank.

HOLLY: There isn't a real tank anyway!

FIN: Holly, if you're going to play with me, you need to play properly.

HOLLY: Look, I'm a mermaid! Look at my long, long hair!

FIN: Who cares about your hair!

HOLLY: I'm Ariel! With my long hair!

> *She sings the Ariel vocal riff, when the character is losing her voice to the sea witch Ursula, in Disney's 1989 animated film* The Little Mermaid *(last section of "Poor Unfortunate Souls").*

FIN: Holly, I'm the Ringleader. If you're the mermaid, just stay in the tank and be quiet.

HOLLY: What tank? There is no tank.

FIN: Just stay on the sofa.

HOLLY: (*mimicking an underwater voice*) I'm a mermaid!!!

> *HOLLY lies on the couch and wiggles her legs in a weak imitation of a mermaid's tail, all while on her phone.*

FIN: Shh! (*as ring leader*) Ladies and Gentlemen, Boys and Girls, pay no attention to the weirdo wriggling in front of you. That's just my sister and she's not supposed to talk if she's a mermaid.

HOLLY: There's nobody out there to hear you.

FIN: But *I* can hear *you* because you're still talking.

> *HOLLY's phone makes notification sounds.*

FIN: Put it on silent. Mermaids don't get texts.

HOLLY: This game's so boring. I'm turning on the TV.

FIN: No! Stop! You're supposed to be quiet.

HOLLY: Not true. There's nothing on Wikipedia about mermaids being quiet. But it does say they all have long, flowing hair. Not weird, short buzz cuts.

FIN: Stop talking about their hair!

HOLLY: Woah, calm down. Jeez!

HOLLY goes back to the game on her phone.

FIN: Why do you even get a phone now?

HOLLY: Cuz I'm in grade seven.

FIN: Not yet.

HOLLY: Well I will be next week. New year, new phone, new Holly.

She takes a selfie.

FIN: You don't seem that new to me.

HOLLY ignores FIN and continues playing around on her phone.

FIN: Holly ...

HOLLY: I'm not listening.

FIN: Except you are, cuz you responded. Holly, do you know what the best part of being a mermaid is?

HOLLY: That they're underwater so they can't hear you?

FIN: No. That they're not a boy or a girl, they're just a mermaid.

HOLLY: I don't care.

FIN: Fine.

HOLLY: Besides, you're wrong, a boy mermaid is a merman.

FIN: No.

HOLLY: It totally is. I just googled it. Like in *The Little Mermaid*, Ariel's dad isn't a mermaid, he's a merman. King Triton!

FIN: For someone who doesn't care, you're sure spending time on it.

HOLLY: That took like five seconds.

FIN: So how do you even know if a mermaid's a boy or a girl?

HOLLY: You can tell.

FIN: How?

HOLLY: Their voice. What they look like. What they're wearing.

FIN: Well they're mostly tail, they don't wear much.

HOLLY: You can tell.

FIN: But can you be sure?

DAD: (*offstage*) Fiona! Holly! Dinnertime!

FIN: Be right down!

HOLLY: Because any kind of animal or creature is either a boy or a girl.

FIN: You should google THAT to make sure.

> HOLLY *exits.* FIN *returns to playing*
> *Ringleader on the coffee table.*

FIN: Step right up, step right up. Because today is a big day. The Doberman Brothers are proud to return with their biggest act to date. A mystical, magnificent transformation. Prepare to be astounded as you see your trusted Ringleader transform into something altogether new: a mermaid.

> *The crowd goes wild.*

Scene Four: Jugglers

MOM: Honey!

DAD: Buddy!

MOM: Sweetheart!

DAD: Fiona!

MOM: Fiona! Where are you?

DAD: Fiona! The food's getting frostbitten.

MOM: Fiona! We're all waiting.

DAD: Fiona! The quicker we eat the quicker we get dessert!

MOM: (*to DAD*) Stuart! (*back to FIONA*) Fiona, I'm hungry.

DAD: Fiona, we're starting without you!

FIN: I'm here!

> *FIN enters the scene with the family.*

MOM: Took you long enough, Fiona. The food's going to be sub-zero by now. We should throw it in the microwave.

FIN: No! Wait!

MOM: Wait for what? We have been waiting! Now just pop it in for a little zap and it will be fine.

FIN: Stop! No!

MOM: What, Fiona? You don't want to eat?

FIN: It's Fin.

MOM: What? What's fin?

FIN: My name. I thought maybe you could start calling me Fin.

Beat. General confusion around the table.

DAD: Fin?

MOM: Fin?

DAD: Like sharks?

MOM: Fin?

DAD: Oh, like Huck Finn?

MOM: You want us to call you Fin?

FIN: Exactly.

DAD: Or Finn from *Adventure Time*!

MOM: But that's not your name. Your name is Fiona.

DAD: It's a beautiful name.

MOM: What's wrong with "Fiona"?

DAD: Good, reliable name!

MOM: You've had that name for nine years.

DAD: More! We chose that name before we even knew we were having a baby.

MOM: We worked hard on that name.

FIN: I think I like Fin.

DAD: Fin. Fin. Fin. Okay, Fin it is.

MOM: Stuart, that's it?! Okay? We're not going to talk about this?

DAD: What is there to talk about? People named Margaret go by Peggy. Elizabeths become Buffy. Fiona becoming Fin makes way more sense!

MOM: But why do you want to change, your name, sweetie? Is there something wrong?

FIN: No, I just ...

MOM: I mean you can tell us anything. Anything at all. You know that, right sweetie?

DAD: Right, buddy?

MOM: Honey, you know that, right?

FIN: (*to the audience*) But I didn't know that. I wanted to ... I ... (*to her parents*) I – I just want to be Fin. Okay?

Scene Five: Clown Interlude I

FIN: Mom didn't get it at first, I don't think.

MOM: She didn't say it at first.

DAD: At first, we thought maybe it was just the name thing.

MOM: How were we supposed to know?

DAD: I knew.

MOM: Stuart, you did not. She was our pride and joy.

DAD: Our baby girl.

MOM: Our little Fiona.

DAD: So different from Holly.

MOM: Siblings are meant to be different.

DAD: Two girls. Same genes, completely and utterly different.

MOM: Holly's the girlie girl. Always has been. I think she was born wearing a tiara.

DAD: And Fiona, our rough and tumble adventurer.

MOM: Nancy Drew.

DAD: Velma from *Scooby-Doo*.

MOM: Hermione from *Harry Potter*.

DAD: Katniss from *The Hunger Games*.

MOM: Stuart! *Harriet the Spy*.

DAD: Not that she spies on us, that's not what we mean.

MOM: Just that they're different. One's yin and one's yang.

DAD: If one says "up," the other says "down."

MOM: Our daughters.

DAD: I had two brothers. Three boys. That was a lot to handle. Let me tell you, my mother was excited to have two granddaughters. To finally have some girls in the family.

MOM: So was I.

DAD: It's not that she doesn't relate to boys, obviously. But girls are ...

MOM: Gentler.

DAD: Really?

MOM: More compassionate.

DAD: Probably.

MOM: Besides, we could use all of Holly's old hand-me-downs and never have to buy Fiona anything.

DAD: Sharon!

MOM: I'm only kidding.

DAD: So when this Fin stuff came up –

MOM: Well I didn't know at first.

DAD: – what it all meant. I mean I knew. I think I did. Deep down.

MOM: Stuart, you didn't. You were just as surprised as –

DAD: I knew something. I had an inkling.

MOM: Uh-huh. She was dressing differently.

DAD: No more Holly hand-me-downs.

MOM: She didn't like the dresses. And she'd never wear pink.

DAD: But neither would you.

MOM: I guess that's true. It's bad with my skin tone.

DAD: But she liked jeans.

MOM: Fiona's always liked jeans.

DAD: Not that that means anything.

MOM: I felt like I'd lost touch with my daughter entirely.

DAD: Girls can wear jeans.

MOM: I know, Stuart, I know.

DAD: So what did we do?

BOTH: We googled it.

DAD: It's not like we didn't know about "transgender" but –

MOM: Until the name thing and the hair incident, I didn't think it applied to our family.

DAD: It's not an "incident," Sharon. I think it's part of his "gender presentation."

MOM: I mean, short hair's in. Maybe she's just a tomboy.

DAD: He's not a tomboy. He's a boy.

MOM: Tomboys are still a thing, aren't they?

DAD: Sure, Sharon, but I don't think that's what we're dealing with here.

MOM: I just didn't know –

DAD: – that Fiona was feeling like Fin. I knew.

MOM: Stuart!

DAD: What?

MOM: Tell me how you knew. When you knew. Because if you knew, why didn't you say anything?

DAD: I don't know when I knew. Maybe it was just a feeling.

MOM: A feeling. Well you never mentioned it. She'd obviously been thinking about it.

DAD: But it wasn't like it happened overnight.

MOM: Well then when was it, Stuart?

DAD: I think this was who Fin had always been.

MOM: Transgender. (*quoting from memory*) "A person whose gender is different from what is expected based on the sex they were assigned at birth." I knew that. I mean I'd read about it, I'm not totally out of touch.

DAD: But then again you're not totally in touch.

MOM: Stuart!

DAD: And that's okay. We're a team!

MOM: I didn't think transgender applied to –

DAD: – Fiona. (*correcting himself*) Fin. My daughter. (*correcting himself*) My son. Fin.

MOM: It's amazing that you've really adopted the name. I'm trying, I am, but it doesn't just roll off the tongue when all I can think is the name Fiona.

DAD: You just have to un-think it. Unlearn it.

MOM: What does that mean?

DAD: That's what Google told me.

MOM: "Unlearn."

DAD: Yes.

MOM: So that's the opposite of "learn"?

DAD: I guess so.

MOM: I'm not going to unlearn my daughter. Why would I want to?

     DAD is reading off his laptop:

DAD: It's a matter of "unlearning our expectations of who our child is based on the gender that we've always seen them as having."

MOM: You spend a lot of time on that computer.

DAD: There's a lot of information to take in. You should take this more seriously.

MOM: I am serious. I'm seriously serious. I'm ... scared. I don't want her life to be harder because of ... All I know is I miss our little girl.

DAD: And that's fair. But she's still there, just differently.

MOM: I guess I'll keep reading.

FIN: (*to the audience*) At five years old, Dad takes us to the circus and something changes. I see these strong women. Women in charge. Not just pretty. Who cares about pretty? Pretty involves wearing things that are too tight, and makeup. My pores like to breathe. Pretty involves uncomfortable shoes.

Ringleader. Bearded Lady. Mermaid. It opens up something that's always been there. This feeling. Knowing something is different but not knowing what it was or how to say it.

Scene Six: Sideshow

HOLLY: So you're Fin now, huh?

FIN: Yup.

HOLLY: Okay. So first your hair's gone and now this.

FIN: Umm, yeah?

HOLLY: You look like you had lice or something.

FIN: I thought it looked okay.

HOLLY: Whatever. So are you, like, my brother now?

FIN: Maybe.

HOLLY: I've never had a brother. But I kind of liked having a sister.

FIN: Did you?

HOLLY: I guess. Yeah. Sort of.

FIN: Well I'm still sort of your sister.

HOLLY: That doesn't make sense.

FIN: Not everything has to make sense all the time. Mermaids don't make sense, but you still love them.

HOLLY: No I don't.

FIN: Right. No more mermaids, just *Candy Crush Saga*.

HOLLY: So, what, I'm supposed to call you Fin now?

FIN: Yeah.

HOLLY: Is that what Mom and Dad said?

FIN: That's what I'm saying.

HOLLY: But school's about to start.

FIN: So?

HOLLY: So what happens then? Do the other kids know?

FIN: Not yet.

HOLLY: Good.

FIN: Good? Why?

HOLLY: It would confuse them.

FIN: Why would that confuse them?

HOLLY: Because you were one thing and now you're something else.

FIN: But I'm still me.

HOLLY: I don't know.

FIN: My teacher doesn't even know yet.

HOLLY: Then don't tell her, okay? It'll be bad enough with everyone seeing your new hair.

FIN: What? Why?

HOLLY: Because it's nobody's business, okay? Nobody needs to know. This isn't *just* about you, okay? It's about all of us. So zip it.

    HOLLY exits.

FIN: (*to the audience*) I didn't know what she meant, really. I thought that telling my family to call me Fin was the most terrifying thing I'd ever done. But once that'd happened, things started feeling easier. Like, once it had all been set in motion, it couldn't be stopped. Like one thing would automatically lead to the next.

Scene Seven: Flying Trapeze

    DAD enters.

DAD: So Fin, are we gonna go throw the ball around in the backyard?

FIN: What?

DAD: Just some father–son bonding time.

FIN: If that's what you want to do.

DAD: Just the boys.

FIN: I've never seen you throw a ball around.

DAD: I guess I've never had anyone to throw it around with.

FIN: You know perfectly well that girls can throw balls too.

DAD: Holly's never much liked sports. I just want to make sure I'm doing the right thing.

FIN: I don't think there is a right thing.

DAD: Probably. So you all ready for the first day of grade four?

FIN: I don't know.

DAD: I thought maybe we could talk through a few things before the craziness of the morning.

FIN: Crazy how?

DAD: In case we're running late like we usually are. What I mean is, do you remember when you were little and I took you to the circus.

FIN: (*to the audience*) He has no idea how important that memory is. (*to DAD*) Doberman Brothers?

DAD: Yeah, exactly. And you remember the trapeze artists flying through the air.

FIN: Yeah, but I mostly remember other stuff.

DAD: Well, do you remember that big webbed blanket that was hanging above the ground just below where the trapeze artists were doing their show?

FIN: Uh, not really. (*to the audience*) Because all I was looking at was the Ringleader, then the Bearded Lady, then the Mermaids, then –

DAD: Well it was there, okay? This big net. And what do you think that was for?

FIN: (*to DAD*) For?

DAD: Well, it's called a "safety net" and it's there to protect them in case –

FIN: – they lose their grip and fall!

DAD: Exactly.

FIN: Okay ...

DAD: Great, you understand.

FIN: I understand what the net's for, but I'm not sure what that has to do with the first day of school.

DAD: Well, a safety net is something that's there to protect someone, to prevent them from getting hurt in case –

FIN: You think I'm going to get hurt?

DAD: No, buddy, of course not. But I think that not everyone understands everything we're going through in the same way that I do.

FIN: Like Mom?

DAD: Mom's finding her way. Don't you worry about Mom.

FIN: So wait, what's the safety net for school?

DAD: Well, I think it's your name.

FIN: Fin?

DAD: No, your original name. Fiona.

FIN: Oh.

DAD: I'm wondering if maybe we can keep the Fin name in our house for now.

FIN: So that at school everyone will call me Fiona. And I'll still be a girl?

DAD: Just for now. But you and I will know that your name's actually Fin.

FIN: And that's for safety?

DAD: I need some time to talk things through with the school. That's all I'm asking for. Time.

FIN: For how long?

DAD: Not long. Just enough to talk to the principal and your teacher so they can talk to the other students. Help them understand and adapt.

FIN: You don't believe me. That I'm Fin and not Fiona.

DAD: Of course I believe you.

FIN: Then why would you ask me to hide?

DAD: What? No, I don't want you to hide. Just to fall safely back on your old name. For now. In case we slip, Fiona is there to catch you.

FIN: Is this about Holly?

DAD: What do you mean?

FIN: I shouldn't have told you. It would have been easier if I kept it to myself.

DAD: No, sweetheart. Please don't say that. I never want you to have to keep things to yourself. I'm glad you told me. And Mom's glad too, it just takes time. That's all I'm saying.

FIN: (*to the audience*) I didn't know what to say. I didn't know what to do. I didn't know anything anymore. I just knew I didn't want morning to come.

Scene Eight: Contortionist

> *General morning sounds: alarm clock, breakfast frying, the morning news on the radio …*

MOM: Honey!

DAD: Buddy!

MOM: Sweetheart!

DAD: Fin!

MOM: We're late!

DAD: Fin, let's get a move on.

MOM: Breakfast is served!

DAD: Fin, hustle buddy!

> *FIN is in his room.*

FIN: I stare in the mirror. I think the hair's good, but what if Holly's right? What if everything's different now, but not good different?

> *He arrives at school.*

FIN: First day of grade four. Everyone's so happy to see each other. Not me. I barely even know these kids. I've been in class with them for three years, but they aren't exactly my friends.

TEACHER: Good morning, boys and girls. Welcome to your first day of class. Hope you've all had a good summer.

CLASS: Yes, miss.

TEACHER: So I don't know about you, but I'm looking forward to all of us getting to know one another. How about everyone begins by telling us something about themselves. Let's start with ... Fiona. Everybody say, "Hi, Fiona."

CLASS: Hi, Fiona.

FIN: Uh, hi. Uh, my name is actually, umm –

CLASS: (*giggling*) Hi, Umm.

FIN: No, I meant that – (*to the audience*) She says:

TEACHER: Fiona, what can you tell me about how you spent your summer? Anything exciting happen? It could be anything: going to the swimming pool, Canada Day fireworks, anything at all.

FIN: But what I hear is:

TEACHER: Fiona, tell us your big secret that you're not allowed to talk about. Because we can all tell that something about you is different. Tell us, we want to hear you say it out loud.

(*to the CLASS, in real life*) Tell you what: how about everybody partners up and together you write fifty words about what you did over the summer. Okay? Everybody got a partner?

FIN: (*to the TEACHER*) Umm, can I go to the bathroom?

> FIN exits and starts to panic.

FIN: I stand in the hall. I want to go into the bathroom, lock myself in a stall, and wait for the bell. But I can't figure out which bathroom to go into. So I stare at both of them, back and forth. I'm about to step into the Boys when a boy comes out –

> FELIX approaches FIN.

FELIX: Hi.

FIN: Hi.

FELIX: Are you going to the bathroom?

FIN: Sort of.

FELIX: I just finished. I even washed my hands. I think you're in my class.

FIN: Okay.

FELIX: Got a partner yet? For the fifty words? Maybe you could be mine.

FIN: Sure.

FELIX: I'm Felix. You're Fiona, right?

FIN: Umm, sort of.

FELIX: What does that mean?

FIN: Umm, nothing.

FELIX: Well then what do I call you?

FIN: I kind of go by Fin.

FELIX: "Fin" like what fish have?

FIN: Yeah, sort of.

FELIX: Oh. Okay. That's cool.

> *FELIX stares at FIN.*

FELIX: Well aren't you going to go into the bathroom?

FIN: I ... No, it's okay. (*to the audience*) We head back to class and I haven't even peed.

FELIX: So what are you gonna write about?

FIN: Huh?

FELIX: What was your favourite part of the summer?

FIN: Well ...

FELIX: Anything cool happen?

FIN: Umm, sort of, but I don't really want to talk about it in front of the class. What about you, what did you do this summer?

FELIX: I took some dance classes. That was pretty good.

FIN: Oh. Like hip hop or something?

FELIX: Something like that.

FIN: Oh, yeah, that's cool.

An awkward pause. FIN tries to get on board.

FIN: I like hip hop.

FELIX: Oh yeah, me too. Who's your favourite rapper?

FIN: Umm – I can't think of them right now.

FELIX: Like, you forgot?

FIN: Yeah.

FELIX: You forgot your favourite rapper?

FIN: Uh-huh.

FELIX: How is that possible?

FIN: I don't know.

FELIX: Are you sure you like rap?

FIN: Not really.

FELIX: Well you don't have to pretend to like something for my sake.

FIN: Oh, okay.

FELIX: I wasn't even taking hip hop.

FIN: Then why did you say you were?

FELIX: Because I don't want everyone to know.

FIN: That you're a dancer?

FELIX: What kind of dance it was.

FIN: (*to the audience*) The teacher says:

TEACHER: Students, you have one minute left to compose your fifty words. Make sure you and your partner are ready to share with the whole class. Everything okay, Fiona?

FIN: But all I hear is:

TEACHER: Do you think all these kids can handle this new version of you? Because they're all about to find out.

FIN: My favourite part of my summer? Finally becoming Fin.

But then the bell rings and I have to change back into Fiona.

Scene Nine: Tightrope Walk

The school bell rings.

FIN: At lunch I sit outside by myself. I thought I might sit with Holly, but she's already reunited with her clique of friends and she's playing double Dutch. (*to invisible legions of fans*) Ladies and Gentlemen, Boys and Girls, my sister Holly and her bevvy of beauties. No longer mermaids, they've sprouted legs and run far away from the shoreline, out of the reach of all the aquatic creatures they used to call friends.

FELIX enters.

FELIX: Hey Fin. What are you doing?

FIN: Nothing.

FELIX: Can I join you?

FIN: Umm ...

FELIX sits.

FELIX: Were you pretending to be in the circus?

FIN: No. Kind of. I don't want to talk about it.

FELIX: What you got for lunch?

FIN: Tuna sandwich.

FELIX: That's weird.

FIN: Why?

FELIX: With the name Fin. It's like you're eating your relatives!

FIN: Ha ha. Right. I didn't think of that.

FELIX: It was just a joke. I've got peanut-butter-and-jelly, but no peanut butter because of the peanut ban.

FIN: So it's just jelly?

FELIX: Yeah, I guess so, but I imagine the peanut butter. Tastes better that way. Your hair's really short.

FIN: So?

FELIX: Nothing. I like it. It's nice.

FIN: Thanks, I did it myself.

FELIX: That's awesome.

FIN: Did you finish writing about your dance class that's not hip hop?

FELIX: Yeah.

FIN: Good.

> *Another awkward pause. These two just can't connect.*

FELIX: Do you want to be friends?

FIN: Umm, I guess so?

FELIX: Because I'm new and I need a friend. And by the looks of things you don't have many.

FIN: I have friends!

FELIX: I don't see them.

FIN: They're just ... busy.

FELIX: So that's why you're sitting all by yourself?

FIN: I was until you got here.

FELIX: If you want me to go away, I'll go.

FIN: No, it's fine.

> *Awkward beat.*

FELIX: It's ballet.

FIN: Huh?

FELIX: The dance classes. I do ballet.

FIN: Oh.

FELIX: Now you're supposed to tell me why you changed your name. And your hair.

FIN: Says who?

FELIX: That's how being friends works. I tell you something about me and then you tell me something about you.

FIN: I'm not supposed to tell anyone.

FELIX: Good thing I don't know anyone.

> *Another awkward beat.*

FELIX: Come on, Fin.

FIN: You really want to know?

FELIX: Yes.

> *FIN can't say it.*

FIN: (*to the audience*) I wanted to tell him. But all I could hear was Holly and Dad saying, "Don't tell anybody," "Keep the Fin name at home." (*to FELIX*) Show me some dance moves?

FELIX: What? Why?

FIN: Because I don't know how to dance at all.

FELIX: Why not? Everyone can dance, you just have to find the beat.

> *He starts doing a ballet demo.* **HOLLY** *arrives, though barely looks up, as she's so involved in her phone.*

HOLLY: Hey! Who's this?

FIN: Oh, this is Felix. Felix, this is my sister Holly.

FELIX: Hi, Holly.

HOLLY: What were you just doing?

FELIX: Umm, nothing.

FIN: We were playing a game.

HOLLY: Oh right, are you Ringleader again?

FIN: No.

FELIX: I was teaching her how to dance.

HOLLY: Looks like someone should be teaching *you* how.

FIN: You're being mean.

HOLLY: Hardly. How's the morning been?

FIN: It's okay.

FELIX: Fin and I had to write about our summer.

> **HOLLY** *looks up from her phone and registers the name.*

HOLLY: Did you say Fin?

FELIX: Uh, yeah.

HOLLY: You told him?

FIN: No ... I ...

FELIX: Umm, I meant Fiona. Right? Fiona. I just said Fin because ... What's going on?

FIN: Nothing.

HOLLY: I told you not to tell people!

FIN: But –

HOLLY: You're unbelievable. And I'm so telling Mom and Dad. You're gonna be sorry. Just you wait till we get home.

>   *HOLLY storms off.*

FELIX: Are you okay?

FIN: Sort of.

FELIX: Why did you tell me to call you Fin if you're not supposed to? I thought you changed your name.

FIN: It's complicated. I wanted to tell you. I needed to tell someone.

FELIX: She seems ... nice.

FIN: Not really.

FELIX: I wish I had a sister.

FIN: Trust me, you don't.

FELIX: Well, a nice sister. Not her.

FIN: Can you do something for me?

FELIX: Maybe.

FIN: Can you call me "he"?

FELIX: What do you mean?

FIN: Earlier you said, "Isn't that her name?" I don't like the words "her" or "she."

FELIX: Oh.

FIN: Yeah. So maybe try "him."

FELIX: But aren't you a girl?

FIN: No, not really.

FELIX: I don't get it. Are you a boy?

FIN: Maybe. Yeah.

FELIX: Oh. I don't really have any friends that are boys. So I guess now we know each other's secrets.

FIN: I guess so.

FELIX: So does that make us friends?

FIN: I guess it does.

FELIX: Good. Now stand up. You're about to learn how to pirouette!

FIN: I don't think so.

FELIX: Don't think about her. Don't think about anything except ballet.

FIN: I've never really thought about ballet in my life.

FELIX: Well then it's time to start.

FIN: Fine. As long as there's no spinning. I might puke if it involves spinning.

FELIX: Just don't puke on me. Ready?

FIN: Ready as I'll ever be.

Scene Ten: Lion Tamer

Later, at home.

HOLLY: Dad, she promised she wouldn't –

DAD: He.

HOLLY: What?

DAD: He, not "she."

HOLLY: So what, the point is he told everyone –

FIN: Not everyone. Just one boy.

HOLLY: – and now everyone's going to find out –

FIN: I don't think Felix will tell anyone.

HOLLY: – and my life is pretty much over.

DAD: Okay, okay, Holly, wait. Calm down, breathe.

HOLLY: Why are you always taking her side?

DAD: His.

HOLLY: "His," whatever. Why do you insist on taking his side when he was the one who broke the rules?

DAD: Holly, we can't have this conversation until you breathe and calm down.

HOLLY: I don't want to breathe, I want everything to be the same as it used to be. I want to lie on the couch and play *Candy Crush Saga* and not have to always talk about how all of a sudden my sister's become my brother and is telling everyone that we have a weird family!

FIN: But I didn't!

HOLLY: What's next? You going to call grandma and tell her? Maybe I should just Snapchat "She's a boy now" and tell the world, since you obviously don't want to keep your mouth shut!

DAD: Holly!

> *HOLLY runs off.*

FIN: It wasn't like I announced it to the class, I –

DAD: I know, Fin, I know.

FIN: I don't want to have to tell people one person at a time. I want them to just know and to just get over it so that I can just be a kid and focus on school and not have to worry so much about whether people know, whether people get it.

DAD: I know.

FIN: Do you? Because if you knew, we wouldn't be waiting, we would be talking to the principal now. We'd be telling the other students now!

DAD: I'm sorry, Fin. You're right. I didn't think it through.

FIN: No, you didn't.

DAD: Let me talk to your mother.

FIN: I told Felix because I needed a friend. That's all.

DAD: I'll talk to your sister.

FIN: Good.

DAD: Now go to sleep.

FIN: Yeah.

DAD: And if you don't want to go to school tomorrow, that's okay. I'll work on this. I promise, it will be okay, buddy. (*beat*) I love you.

FIN: I know.

> FIN *exits.* MOM *arrives.*

MOM: Going to sleep?

DAD: Soon.

MOM: Rough day?

DAD: The days aren't getting easier.

MOM: Well it's all a lot to take in. I mean she's just a kid.

DAD: Yes, he's a kid, but he's a kid that feels very strongly about something and we need to understand that. And respect that.

MOM: I can't help but think that if only I'd –

DAD: What, done more feminine things with him? Look at Holly. She's so purely and completely herself. Isn't it only right that we afford Fin the same luxury? Fin has asked us to understand that he's a boy.

MOM: I know. I know that. You're not the only one reading things.

DAD: I'm really happy to hear that. Because it's one thing for you to be scared. Let's be scared with each other, and then let's be brave for Fin. Because he can't be the only brave one.

MOM: All I want to do is be a good mom.

DAD: Good, then be one.

MOM continues her laptop research.

Scene Eleven: Clown Interlude II

FIN: (*to the audience*) I don't remember when I was little. Obviously. But my mom always said I was a "brave" girl. I would do the things that Holly was too scared to do. And they weren't even dangerous. Maybe just gross. Pick up dog poop in the backyard. Dig holes in the backyard for Dad to plant a new hedge. I could never understand why those things were brave. They felt like the kinds of things you do when your mom asks you to. I didn't realize until later that that's not how a girl's supposed to act.

DAD: Are you coming to bed?

MOM: I wish ... I don't know what I wish. That she would have told me.

DAD: "He."

MOM: Fine. Yes. He. So many changes. Heck, I remember I used to be a goth.

DAD: You were never a goth!

MOM: Sure I was. In grade ten.

DAD: You just dyed your hair black. That didn't make you a goth.

MOM: You know what I'm saying.

DAD: I don't know that I do. I mean are you comparing the two? Are you honestly saying that you dyeing your hair is the same as our child telling us that –

We enter an earlier memory.

FIN: (*to MOM and DAD*) I'm not a girl. I'm a boy. I've always been a boy. You just haven't been paying attention. I didn't know how to tell you. I didn't want to upset you. But I need you to know that. So that ... I don't know what. So that you know that. It's not just my hair and my name, it's –

DAD: It's okay, Fin, we love you.

MOM: We love you regardless, Fiona.

FIN: It's Fin.

MOM: Fin. Yes. I'm sorry, love. I'm sorry.

FIN: (*to the audience*) But all I hear is:

MOM: Where did my daughter go? Why are you taking her away and leaving me with –

DAD: (*back in reality*) Fin, we will do whatever you need us to do to support you –

MOM: Whatever you need, so long as we keep it within the family. Right?

FIN: But I can't just hop back in the family boat!

We exit the memory and are back to the present.

DAD: What's with you?

MOM: Well, I can't be expected to be fine with it overnight. I mean she's known about herself for a while. This is new for me. And I'm trying to catch up. That's all.

DAD: He and himself.

MOM: Yes, he. (*beat*) I love him so much, but I need time.

DAD: But he needs a mother.

MOM: These things happen in phases, and who knows, tomorrow, she, he might –

DAD: Do you honestly think our daughter Fiona becoming Fin, "she" becoming "he" is a phase?

MOM: Well I was once a vegetarian.

DAD: Oh c'mon, Sharon, open your eyes.

MOM: That's easy for you to say. All of a sudden she's your son.

DAD: He!

MOM: Oh knock it off. You know I'm trying.

DAD: I don't know that, actually. So try harder. And when we mess up we apologize and we try again. Even harder.

MOM: Why is this so easy for you?

DAD: The better question is, why is it hard for you?

MOM: What am I missing?

DAD: You're missing that he's our kid. And it's our job to make this easier for him.

Scene Twelve: Human Cannonball

FIN: (*to the audience*) It's not that Mom wasn't trying. It's just that things aren't always easy. They weren't for her and they weren't for …

DAD: Holly, honey!

> *Beat.*

DAD: Holly, sweetheart.

Beat.

DAD: Holly?

After a moment, DAD knocks.

DAD: Can I come in?

HOLLY: No!

DAD: Please? Holly, we've got to talk.

HOLLY: We are talking!

DAD: You know what I mean. Talking face to face.

HOLLY: Why?

DAD: You know exactly why.

HOLLY: So you can tell me I'm wrong and say that Fin's right?

DAD: It's more complicated than that.

HOLLY: Everything's always complicated when it comes to Fiona.

DAD: Fin.

HOLLY: I know, I was making a point.

DAD: I'm coming in, Holly.

DAD enters.

HOLLY: I'm allowed to have an opinion.

DAD: I'm not saying you can't.

HOLLY: I'm allowed to not like what he did. We don't talk about everything everywhere. Some things stay at home.

DAD: Holly –

HOLLY: I'm allowed to not like it. I'm allowed to miss my sister and to want things to be normal again and not have everything revolve around who Fin is. Why can't I go to school like a normal kid and worry about a quiz instead of worrying about people finding out that my sister's a boy now?

DAD: Holly –

HOLLY: And it's not like it's even my fault. You're the one who told Fin that we shouldn't talk about it at school and then he did. But you didn't even get mad at him for doing the exact thing you told him not to do.

DAD: Holly –

HOLLY: And I know what you're going to say, you're going to say I have to be more sensitive and I have to support him and I have to understand, and maybe I don't want to, okay?

DAD: Are you finished?

HOLLY: Did you hear what I said?

DAD: Yes, I heard you.

HOLLY: Okay. And?

DAD: And I think you're right.

HOLLY: Really?

DAD: Yes. I did tell Fin not to talk about it. I admit that.

HOLLY: Okay.

DAD: But that wasn't the right thing to do. Sometimes parents make decisions and then only later do we realize that it wasn't the right one. And then it's too late. But I'm trying to fix this. And I want you to fix this with me.

HOLLY: So why do I have to be the one to fix it? Why can't Fin?

DAD: Look, I'm not saying it's going to be easy immediately. And I'm not telling you that you have to understand everything right away. But I've noticed that you're doing a really good job with calling him Fin. That's being a great big sister. So I'm asking for your help. And for you to be patient. Both with me and with Fin. And your mom too. And I promise that I'll be patient too. I know that everything isn't going to change overnight –

HOLLY: I think it already did!

DAD: – so what I need from you is a promise that we will take things one day at a time, and that we will talk about them as a family. Because this isn't about Fin, this is about all of us. The whole family. And if the whole family isn't in the boat –

HOLLY: I'm not saying it, Dad.

DAD: Please?

HOLLY: (*reluctantly*) If the whole family isn't in the boat, then it starts to sink instead of float.

DAD: Exactly. I love you sweetie. And I know you're frustrated, but everything's gonna get easier.

Scene Thirteen: Fire Breathing

FIN: Some things in life play out a thousand times in my head like a movie on a loop. Over and over. Different moments that replay and I try to figure out if any of them point toward a beginning. I don't know when it started, but I know that it never really ended.

The bell rings. The **TEACHER** *dismisses the class.*

TEACHER: That's it for today, class. Fiona, can you stay behind for a second?

FIN walks over to the TEACHER.

TEACHER: Fiona, I couldn't help but notice that you only wrote twenty words instead of fifty.

FIN: Oh. Really?

TEACHER: I think you know very well that "I had a great summer. We did lots of things. The days were really hot. The air conditioning was cold" only adds up to twenty words. And you didn't really explain anything specific. See, I've caught on to your little secret, and it's only a matter of time until everyone else knows too.

> *FIN wakes up. It was just a dream.*
> *He hasn't actually returned to school.*

FIN: (*to the audience*) But it's just a dream. I didn't even go to school the next day. I couldn't.

> *There's a knock at the door. It's FELIX.*

FELIX: Hey Fin.

FIN: What are you doing here?

FELIX: You weren't at school. I got worried.

FIN: I can't talk right now.

FELIX: Oh.

> *He does his best to be absent, but is very noticeable.*

FELIX: I'm not very good at not talking.

FIN: I noticed.

FELIX: Can I ask you something?

FIN: No.

FELIX: Why does the teacher still call you Fiona?

FIN: What do you mean?

FELIX: She was doing attendance this morning and she called "Fiona." I didn't say anything, but it was weird.

He tries hard not to speak. It's no use.

FELIX: Can I ask you something else?

FIN: No.

FELIX: Like if you have to pee at school what bathroom do you use?

FIN: I said I don't want to talk about it.

FELIX: Come on, that was a whole other question.

FIN: Well I don't want to talk about it either. I don't want to answer questions, okay? It's none of your business where I pee anyway!

FELIX: Did I say something wrong?

FIN: Yes!

FELIX: I'm sorry!

FIN: I don't care! Just stop talking! Why are you even here? You shouldn't have come.

FELIX starts to leave.

FIN: Do you know how exhausting it is to have to constantly correct people?

FELIX: Not really.

FIN: Imagine if every time someone said your name they called you Helix instead.

FELIX: Helix is kind of an awesome name.

FIN: Stop joking! Not everything's a joke, okay?

FELIX: I know that. I get it.

FIN: Do you? How hard could your life possibly be?

FELIX: Oh, you think it's fun being the Ballerina Boy? Yesterday someone asked me how I fit a tutu in my backpack.

FIN: So? That's not that same thing.

FELIX: And there's a kid in grade six who glares at me at recess. I don't even want to go outside because he just stares and stares and I don't know what he's going to do.

FIN: It's not the same thing, Felix. Not even close!

FELIX: No, it's not. But it doesn't mean I don't feel it. Just because you're going through stuff, it doesn't mean my feelings don't exist.

FIN: I can't be myself at school.

FELIX: Well, neither can I. Not exactly.

FIN: You can NOT do ballet at school. I can't NOT be a boy! You really don't get it, do you?

FELIX: I'm doing my best.

FIN: Well maybe your best isn't good enough!

   Beat.

FELIX: So are we going to hang out? We could play circus or something.

FIN: No. I want to be alone.

FELIX: Fine. Whatever you want. Maybe you're right and I don't understand everything right away. But it doesn't mean I'm not trying. And I can't help you if you're going to be like this about it. So stop taking it out on the people who want to be your friend.

Scene Fourteen: Ventriloquist

> *FIN enters.*

MOM: Fin!

FIN: What?

MOM: Come here for a sec.

FIN: Where's Dad?

MOM: He had a meeting. How about you sit down.

FIN: Am I in trouble?

MOM: Not at all.

FIN: Then what?

MOM: Well, there's something I need to do, and I'd rather that we do it together.

FIN: Is it laundry?

MOM: No.

FIN: Dishes?

MOM: No, it's not a chore.

FIN: Okay.

MOM: I need your help to write something.

FIN: You don't know how to write?

MOM: Of course I know how to write. But I want help from my son.

FIN registers that she's said "son" for the first time.

FIN: Oh. Okay.

MOM starts writing.

MOM: "Dear Family, Friends, and Colleagues. I am writing this letter to share with you some news about our family." (*to FIN*) So far so good?

FIN: Yeah.

MOM: "I am the proud mother of a transgender son, and I am hoping in sharing this with you that you can help become part of the network of adults who will make him feel safe and loved every day ..."

FIN is overwhelmed hearing his mom refer to him as her son.

Scene Fifteen: Finale

FIN: So that was it. That was the story of how I came out. Or something like that anyway. And the best part? Turns out the circus is coming to town even more often. It's different now, but the costumes only get better. And you know what? Most of the time I can't even tell who's a boy and who's a girl.

FELIX enters.

FELIX: Hey Fin.

FIN: Hey Felix. It's good to see you.

FELIX: Yeah?

FIN: Yeah. I'm really sorry.

FELIX: Cool.

FIN: You want to play circus?

FELIX: I really do.

FIN: You can be the Ringleader if you want.

FELIX: No, I think you should be. Cuz I brought you something.

FELIX pulls out a proper Ringleader costume.

FIN: WOAH! This is amazing.

FELIX: Put it on.

FIN does.

FIN: It's perfect. Thank you.

FELIX: Thank you, too.

FIN: For what?

FELIX: I don't know. Just cuz.

FIN smiles.

FIN: Step right up, step right up. See Dad the Lion Tamer in his bravest move yet! See Mom, the contortionist trying to figure out how to get through this dangerous minefield. See Holly, the mermaid swimming in silence, and Felix the Ballerina Boy twirling on the tightrope. And me? I'm Fin. Full beard and top hat. Maybe I'm the Bearded Lady. Maybe I'm another mermaid. But I'm definitely Ringleader. So pay attention. Ladies and Gentlemen, Boys and Girls, and everyone in between. Welcome to the Greatest Show on Earth!

ACKNOWLEDGMENTS

Nelly Boy was written with support from the Ontario Arts Council's Theatre Creators' Reserve, as well as from the Canada Council for the Arts.

Thanks to Christine Horne, Jason Lambert, Cole Alvis, Jason Hand, Laura Gardner, Jaclyn Zaltz, Steven Jackson, and Jason Sharman for their work on the workshop production.

Special thanks to Lynda Hill and Cameron Mackenzie for their stewardship of the play in its various forms.

My Funny Valentine was commissioned by Zee Zee Theatre and developed through the Playwrights Theatre Centre's Playwrights Colony, with dramaturgical support from Don Hannah and Heidi Taylor. Zee Zee continued supporting its development through three productions. Thank you to Kyle Cameron for his tremendous character insights as well as later cast members Anton Lipovetsky and Conor Wylie. Additional thanks to Jay Whitehead at Theatre Outré, Evalyn Parry at Buddies in Bad Times Theatre, Neil Scott at Centre Stage at Surrey City Hall, and Sean Guist at Intrepid Theatre's OUTstages Festival.

Thanks to Adam Barrett and Cameron Mackenzie for their devotion to the play's earliest drafts.

Ladies and Gentlemen, Boys and Girls was written with the support of a Playwright-in-Residency Grant at Roseneath Theatre through the Canada Council for the Arts.

Special thanks to the tremendous community of trans and queer folx and incredible allies who enabled this play to come into the world: Rae Takaesu, Sunny Drake, Samson Brown, Andrew Lamb, Annemieke Wade, Gretel Meyer Odell, Nicole Mitchell, Courtney Pyke, Stephanie Jung, Meryn Caddell, and JP Kane.

Overall none of these plays would have ever made it to the stage, let alone a book, without the unwavering support of Janina and Dennis Deveau, Cameron Mackenzie, Deborah Williams, and the late Jon Kaplan.

DAVE DEVEAU investigates queer themes that speak to a broad audience. His work has been produced across North America and in Europe. He is the playwright-in-residence for Vancouver's Zee Zee Theatre, who produced his plays *Nelly Boy, Tiny Replicas, My Funny Valentine* (winner of the Sydney J. Risk Prize for Outstanding Original Play by an Emerging Playwright, nominated for a Jessie Richardson Theatre Award and an Oscar Wilde Award), *Lowest Common Denominator, Elbow Room Café: The Musical* (with Anton Lipovetsky), and *Dead People's Things*. His first three plays for young audiences were all commissioned and premiered with Green Thumb Theatre, and have subsequently continued into other productions: *Out in the Open, tagged* (Dora Mavor Moore Award nomination), and *Celestial Being* (Jessie Richardson Theatre Award nomination). He is devoted to developing intelligent, theatrical plays for young people that foster conversation. In total, his plays have been nominated for twenty-one Jessie Richardson Theatre Awards, four Ovation Awards, and four Dora Mavor Moore Awards. When not creating plays, he is performing for audiences of all ages and spectrums under the name Peach Cobblah, and raising his beautiful son with his husband Cameron.

www.davedeveau.com

Author photo by Brandon Gaukel